The

# of Phenloris

An Adventure in a Magical Land

Therese Grant

Mary Sue! Thank you for all
your support & prayers. Your friend Teri
Love

T. Grant
7/3/14

Brighton Publishing LLC
435 N. Harris Drive
Mesa, AZ 85203

The Fairy Clan of Phenloris

An Adventure in a Magical Land

Therese Grant

Brighton Publishing LLC
435 N. Harris Drive
Mesa, AZ 85203

www.BrightonPublishing.com

ISBN 13: 978-1-62183-166-2
ISBN 10: 1-62183-166-3

Printed in the United States of America

First Edition

Cover Design: Tom Rodriguez

Dedication

To my husband, Christopher, whose constant help and encouragement never fails to inspire me.

Acknowledgements

I would like to thank two great friends who happen to be teachers—Helen Lathrop and Eileen Sullivan. I would never have started this adventure in writing without their help and continued support.

A special thanks to my family who never stopped asking, "Are you done yet?"

I would like to give a big thank you to my choir family, who are the kindest of people. They are always generous with their friendship and prayers.

Last, but certainly not least, Kathie McGuire, my publisher, who gives more than she receives. I would not be where I am today if not for you, Kathie; and to her editing staff as well. All of you are awesome!

Character's Phonetic Pronunciations Key

Ahthuwin .... (ath-oo-win)

Aredoe .... (air-a-doe)

Arnault .... (are-nalt)

Bardfey .... (bar-d-fay)

Bonneisse .... (bon-niece)

Cassahandra .... (kaasa-hand-rah)

Coremerick .... (corr-mear-ick)

Diafiena .... (die-a-fe-nah)

Dolbatheryn .... (dole-bath-earn)

Egwin .... (egg-win)

Ellennin .... (el-en-inn)

Gauwain .... (gah-wayne)

Gilthew .... (gill-thuoo

Glenlillian .... (glen-lilly-en)

Inisgoud .... (in-ess-good)

Jahaziel .... (ha-see-el)

Karapalis .... (kear-a-pall-iss)

Kimberlyn .... (kim-burr-len)

Lembath .... (leem-bath)

Llanider .... (lee-and-er)

Lutherian .... (loo-thear-ean)

Meirionwen .... (mary-on-wen)

Merddlyn .... (myrtle-lin)

Mirrororme .... (meer-or-me)

Newery .... (noo-ree)

Oneth .... (own-th)

Phenloris .... (fen-lore-es)

Sharron .... (share-on)

Siomara .... (see-a-mara)

Prologue

Long ago, in a land no longer remembered, lived a clan of fairies well-hidden from men and kings. Their peaceful existence went undisturbed and unnoticed until…

PART ONE

The Golden Chalice

Chapter One

The fairy stood motionless next to the man lying on the ground. He was not breathing. Blood was oozing slowly from a wound in his left shoulder where an arrow protruded. She could not remember being this close to one, and this gave her pause. She cautiously knelt down near his face to get a better look.

When his eyelids flickered, she jumped back and then fluttered her wings until she rose a foot above him.

He was alive.

Quickly looking around for other humans, she was relieved to see they were alone.

Who could have done such a terrible thing? Did they think they had killed him? she wondered. Sadly, she had no answer to these questions, and she slowly lowered herself back down to the ground.

The fairy placed her hand on the man's forehead, brushing the overly long, dark, auburn hair away from his face. She said a soft prayer for safety before she flew to find help. Her wings stretched out, and she called the wind to gently cover the man with leaves, hiding him until she returned with her mother.

Sir Jahaziel, knight and captain of the guard of the newly crowned king, did not dare move for fear of scaring the fairy away. She was speaking to the wind, and he could hear and see the leaves moving quickly to do her bidding. Before he was completely covered, he smiled, content that his last moments on this earth had been spent seeing the most beautiful creature he had ever laid eyes upon. It was his last thought before he passed out from the pain and exhaustion.

"How many times have I told you to stop walking around everywhere? You have wings for a reason, Kim. I promise you, one day in the near future, I will be horrified to find some creature eating you for its dinner because you are so careless." Glenlillian, crystal fairy mother, ended her words to her daughter with great emphasis.

"I am too fast to be caught by anyone or anything," Kim mumbled.

"Is that boasting I hear coming from your lips, young lady?" her mother challenged.

"No, Mother," Kim answered, smiling. She continued collecting the things needed to help the injured man, who had somehow managed to enter their forest before he fell unconscious.

As Kim and Glenlillian pulled down the dried healing herbs that hung from the braided morning glory rope in the hot room of their home, Glenlillian decided to speak of other things. As a healer, she knew the task at hand would be difficult because of the sheer size of the man.

"Now that you and Huw are promised, we must consider planning your acceptance gathering," Kim's mother said.

Kim held the sack open for her mother, and Glenlillian filled it to capacity.

"Mother, we have plenty of time for that. You know as well as I that Huw was waiting for his promotion. He trained hard to be elected first guard to father, and he wanted this task behind him before agreeing to the gathering. Besides, we decided to wait for the blooming of the cherries before throwing such a festival," Kim said.

"Oh, Sweetling, that is a wonderful choice. Picking the spring solstice for the festivities will add so much more excitement. I can't wait to start planning," her mother replied.

Satisfied she had everything needed to heal the man, Glenlillian spoke once again. "Let us go and do this before darkness falls. Your father and Huw will be home tomorrow, and I do not dare think what Luther would say or do if he were here."

They flew back to where the injured human lay.

"Make him drink all of that liquid, Kim. I can see he is in terrible pain," Glenlillian said, as she pointed to the large baked clay pot on the ground that was filled with an ancient elixir. She continued tearing strips of cloth.

As she knelt once again next to the human, Kim spoke quietly into his ear. "Sir, you must drink this potion, for it will ease your pain. My mother must remove the arrow from your shoulder before she can pack the wound with our special herbs for healing. Can you hear me?"

Kim held the man's face in her small hands waiting for him to answer. When she heard his strained "yes," Kim looked at her mother and nodded.

Sir Jahaziel fell into a deep sleep and dreamed of a beautiful fairy laughing and smiling at him. Her long, blonde hair moved slightly with the breeze, and shone in varied shades when the sun peeked through the slowly moving clouds. In his dream, they were well-acquainted with each other and appeared to be good friends. The fairy was handing him a key, and he was telling her how fortunate they were to find it.

Then the pain hit him, and he sat up quickly trying to stop the person responsible for his torture. His roar was deafening.

Kim held his face again and yelled as loud as she could for

the knight to stop moving. "Please, sir, do not move around. You will start bleeding again. My mother and I are near exhaustion from tending you," she exclaimed.

Jahaziel opened his eyes and looked directly at the beautiful fairy hovering so close to his face. Then he spoke in a hoarse, raspy voice, "If you tell me your name, I will not move."

Kim's huge smile had Jahaziel smiling in response.

"My name is Kimberlyn, but my family uses the shorter version, Kim. You may address me so. I am the one who found you. My mother has gone to brew you a healing tea of honeysuckle, rosemary, and chamomile. It hides the taste of the potion you will need to drink, and it will calm you. This tea will also help you gain your strength quickly, and you should be able to stand within the hour," she told him.

Kim eased herself back. She pointed down to the ground at a very large leaf with a coiled cloth inside.

"I must wrap your shoulder with this cloth. I warn you, however, it smells awful and it will burn the damaged area. It is specially made for closing wounds and stopping blood flow. We do not use hot irons like my mother has witnessed people doing, because she finds that to be a cruel practice. Also, my mother said this cloth will slowly disappear, so there will be no need to remove it," Kim explained.

When she received his nod, she lifted the cloth and began winding it around his shirtless, wounded shoulder. Steam rose from the cloth and made a noise like meat searing on a spit. Jahaziel jerked slightly, and he pounded hard on the ground with his right fist.

By the time Kim finished the wrap, she was shaking. Tears fell from her periwinkle blue eyes, and drifted slowly down her face. When Jahaziel saw them, he reached up with his right hand, placed his fingers at the back of her head, and gently wiped at her tears with his thumb. Kim was so shocked at his touch that she could not move, and her breath caught in her lungs. Now, because of his touch, a bond was formed, set, and unbreakable.

Satisfied her tears had stopped, Jahaziel spoke. His deep baritone voice was clear and steady. "I can see this has distressed you, and I am thankful to you and your mother for your kindness. I believe you have saved my life, and I am now honor-bound to both of you."

His smile calmed Kim, and he continued speaking. "My name is Jahaziel. I am knight and captain of King Crawford's guard. I was attacked by a man known as the Black Knight, who seeks a great treasure for his king—a golden chalice he believes has great power that he desires for his own gain. He was told King Crawford is in possession of this chalice, and he attacked Fitzhuwlyn Castle. When he and his men realized they would be defeated, they ran. I was chasing the Black Knight through the meadow. I was struck down near this area when he changed course and headed in the direction of King Crawford's forest.

"If you live here, you and your family must be very careful, for I heard he plans to burn this forest to the ground in retaliation for his defeat. When King Crawford hears of this I will suggest he set guards around the perimeter to ensure this does not happen. However, we cannot be everywhere at every moment. Do you understand me, Kim?" he asked.

Kim nodded.

They turned at the sound of Glenlillian's approach.

"Let us see if you can stand, Sir Jahaziel," Glenlillian spoke in a firm voice. She motioned for Kim to assist her.

Jahaziel shook his head slightly as he thought, *Until today I had not considered the possibility that fairies existed.*

He could not believe they were mother and daughter, so opposite in appearance—from the darkest to the lightest of hair, and the palest-blue to the blackest-of-black eyes. And Kim was nearly a foot taller than her mother, a trait she received from her father's side of the family.

The fairies held on to Jahaziel's hands, and pulled him to a standing position. He was surprised at their strength. He swayed slightly, and then gained a steadier foothold. His shoulder was sore and stiff, and his steps were slow and awkward. This brought thoughts to his mind of a very old man he knew.

"I need to get back to the castle quickly before darkness falls. Do you think you can help me gain my horse?" Jahaziel asked.

"We have seen no horse, Sir Jahaziel," Glenlillian spoke.

Jahaziel put two fingers to his mouth, and then whistled. A moment passed—two, three. The sound of his horse approaching broke the silence, and everyone laughed.

Steadily seated on his massive, silver-spotted destrier, Jahaziel thanked both fairies for their help, and then turned to leave. Turning back around, he motioned for Kim to come to him.

He reached into a pocket of his torn jacket, and pulled out a long, delicately made silver chain that had a silver ring hanging from it. He broke the chain, removed the ring, and then handed it to her.

"This is a family ring, forged and given to each first-born male when he turns of age. These rings are passed down generation to generation and have my family crest engraved on the inside. Do you see the half moon, sun, and star just here?" he said, as he pointed to the inscribed image.

Kim leaned closer to look, and then nodded her head.

"It symbolizes our family motto, 'Till waning sun and moon be no more, we search the heavens for strength to first seek justice.' I give this to you as a gift and as a sign of distress. If you are ever in need of my assistance for any reason, send this to me. I will come to you as soon as I am able," he told her.

Kim could only nod, so stunned at receiving such a precious gift. She squeezed Jahaziel's ring over the fingers of her left hand, placing it securely onto her wrist. Jahaziel smiled at her, nodded, turned around, and set his horse into a run.

They smiled at Jahaziel's parting words. "Thank you for the teas, Glenlillian. They were most refreshing."

Glenlillian glided over to her daughter, lifted her arm and looked at the gift Jahaziel had given her. "I believe this means you are engaged to be married," she said.

Both fairies burst out laughing and headed for home.

Chapter Two

Jahaziel stood near the large fireplace in the receiving hall of Fitzhuwlyn Castle, awaiting his king's reply. He tried to be patient, absently rubbing his left shoulder in an attempt to take the sting from it. King Crawford knew everything that had occurred in regard to the Black Knight, and Jahaziel's subsequent wounding. He assured Jahaziel that royal guards would be placed around the forest area to be certain there would be no burning.

Then Jahaziel asked if he knew of the fairies.

After long moments passed in silence, the king spoke.

"I have heard stories of fairies, but I have not looked upon such creatures. You say that one is quite tall for a fairy? Have you seen many fairies, Jahaziel?" he asked.

Jahaziel laughed, a full rich sound, and admitted this was his first encounter. He showed the king their approximate size by placing his hand just above his knee.

The king continued, "Why do you suppose they are here? I do not recall being told about them as a child. There must be a reason they have suddenly decided to show themselves."

"I have only heard rumors, sire, and, like everyone else, I thought that most were children's tales," the knight said.

The king nodded his acceptance of Jahaziel's answer, and then turned back to the topic of the Black Knight.

He was called the Black Knight because he was as black in

hair and eyes as his clothes, horse, sword, shield, and attitude. The king and Jahaziel had heard rumors that he had been killed in the battle of Newry along with his king, King Arnault. But, they were only rumors, and obviously untrue.

“Sire, what is King Arnault’s story? What does he have against you that he would lie and summon an army to take from you what you do not possess?” Jahaziel asked.

Tiredness came over the king as he recalled what he knew of King Arnault.

“It all began twelve years ago. King Edward held court several times at Allenwood Castle. I am sure you heard the rumors about the large, lavish, social gatherings he and Queen Lenore held to attract a husband for their daughter, Princess Joyce,” King Crawford said.

Jahaziel nodded.

“Although Joyce was only twelve at the time, the engagement would ensure lands and other holdings would go to the couple upon King Edward’s death. Arnault was one of many suitors who tried to persuade King Edward to agree to the engagement and marriage,” the king continued.

“Edward knew of Arnault’s reputation, and refused many times. Arnault became enraged, insisting on a joust for the favor of Joyce. By summons, my father, King George, was asked to attend this gathering since he and Edward were great friends. Edward stated in the summons he was in need of his counsel. My father was still recovering from illness and was told to remain at Fitzhuwlyn Castle. He was told not to travel even the short distance between there and Allenwood. Edward did not know me very well, only having visited us on a few occasions, but he trusted my father and, therefore, trusted me. I was given the honor to fight on behalf of King Edward,” King Crawford recalled.

He laughed heartily. “At twenty two, I was not of a mind to

marry, but less inclined to allow Arnault to get his hands on Joyce. So I agreed."

The king continued, "The jousting tournament brought many onlookers from many lands around the area. It boosted Arnault's ego. He was so arrogant and assured of his win, he sent a few servants ahead. By his command, they had gathered some of his personal things to bring back to Allenwood."

"I injured Arnault on the third pass. My lance went into the bone of his left leg, causing him to fall hard from his horse, breaking his right arm in the process. Edward's physicians were in attendance and saved his life, but Arnault was left with pain and a noticeable limp," King Crawford said, pausing in thought.

"My concerns," the king finally continued, "are in understanding where this knight acquired his information that I am in possession of this golden chalice. What was so important that Arnault had shown himself, and was willing to risk war between our neighbors to possess it? And what was its significance? You have shown me time and time again that I can trust you, Jahaziel. I have decided to put you in charge. Find the answers to my questions. But, understand me, this is to be done as quietly as possible. You are to do whatever you feel is necessary to gain this information. My hope is in finding that no such chalice exists, and that this Black Knight is mistaken."

"If you are in agreement, sire, I think I should take some of King Edward's men with me," Jahaziel said. "Although I go back and forth from Allenwood to here, the men need more practice. They grow lax and weak of muscle when I am not in attendance. Since the death of King Edward last year, a deep sadness remains within its walls, and his people grow lazy. His men and knights like me well enough, and did not oppose your decision to assign me as regent, but I worry that their continued grieving will cause infighting and unnecessary bickering. I think it would be good for them to go on a quest with me."

"Yes, Jahaziel, I agree you should take Edward's men as well as a few of mine. I await your report," King Crawford said.

Jahaziel nodded to his king, and then left the castle in search of answers.

While she picked the daisies that her mother had asked for, Kim looked at her bracelet ring, admiring how it shone in the sun. The daisies would make a splendid tea, according to her mother, and would make a fairy strong.

Suddenly, Lulu Piggy wobbled over to her and stopped at her feet.

"Oh, hello, Lulu. What are you doing all the way over here? Is it not a far walk from your burrow to this meadow?" Kim remarked.

Lulu Piggy had something important to tell Kim, and she spoke with rushed words.

The guinea pig told Kim what she had heard from a large man on a big horse talking to another man in a huge wagon. The man on the horse was asking the man in the wagon a lot of questions about something he was trying to find. Lulu did not understand what he was saying. The wagon man did not want to answer. He seemed afraid of the large man and his horse. The wagon man excused himself, and quickly left. Lulu thought this was important, and told Kim so.

"Have you seen this wagon man before?" Kim asked.

Lulu gave her a "yes," and told Kim where she had seen him.

"I see, so he comes and goes from that large castle north of here?" Kim asked.

Lulu answered, "Yes," again.

"What about the big man? Have you seen him before?" Kim continued to question Lulu.

Lulu's clearly stated "no," told Kim that Lulu was getting upset. So, she decided to end the conversation.

"Thank you for this information, Lulu. I promise to look into this. If there is a problem, I know someone who may be able to help," Kim told the little guinea pig.

Satisfied with Kim's words, Lulu quickly walked in the direction of her home.

Kim smiled to herself thinking about what a nosy little guinea pig Lulu was, and how she always managed to blow everything out of proportion. Lulu's lineage was impressive. She was the eighth generation in a line of very nosy and nervous guinea pigs.

While Kim walked back to her home she continued to pick daises along the way. She smiled at the memory of her first guinea pig sighting.

She had been just a baby when she met her first guinea pigs. Counting on her fingers she said aloud, "There were Harriet and Horace, a very outspoken couple, and extremely comical, if I ever saw one. Let me see…then Paula and George, Peppy and Micamica, Schroder and Gail, Weezee and Wilma, Gizmoz and Lillian, Sidney and Blue, and finally, Marshall and Lulu."

Kim laughed at the memory. With her sack filled to overflowing, she headed for home.

Mumbling to herself, she said, "I wonder if I should find Jahaziel and tell him what Lulu has told me."

Kim knew her mother did not want her speaking to Sir Jahaziel, so she thought up a plan to meet with him and tell him that some kind of trouble was about to come. Her insight told her something was amiss, but she knew not what.

Glenlillian knew her husband was angry. He did not like hearing they had tended a wounded male human alone without an elfin guard, let alone had a conversation with him. His hands were behind his back, and he was flitting back and forth from window to hearth in their well-hidden home among the Cypress trees.

Kim flew in and spotted her father. He stopped at seeing her enter, and turned toward her. Prepared for the onslaught, he opened his arms wide. In only one fairy moment, Kim dropped her daisies, and slammed into her father so hard that she knocked them into the soft mud wall of the crafting room.

"Father!" she hollered, and then hugged him so hard he expelled his breath.

Lutherian, woodland guard fey king and father of Kim, had a smile on his face. The love he had for his daughter shone brightly in his eyes.

"What have you been feeding our child, Glen?" Kim's father asked his wife. "She is nearly as tall as I am, and squeezes me like my best-trained guard, Huw."

Kim laughed at her father. Then she looked at her mother. Her smile slowly faded, and she knew her mother had told on them.

"How has this Black Knight heard of our golden chalice?" Lutherian asked.

Kim knew when her father spoke soft and low he was truly angry.

Luther continued, "All fey guards of this clan have taken great pains to ensure no human would know of our honored chalices when we moved from Phenloris to this area. The journey for all of us was long and difficult after the great fire, but someone must have spoken to this knight. Our law is sacred, and we are honor-bound to not interfere or have contact with humans!"

Luther ended his statement with a roar, and turned once again to the hearth, hoping it would calm him.

Glenlillian spoke to her husband with soft words while touching his shoulder. "Kim has the gift of kindness, Luther. You know as well as I how rare this is at birth. She cannot help her nature, and she would have made herself ill had she not tended the knight. We decided it was best to heal him and send him on his way."

Luther went to his daughter, lifted her left arm, which still had the ring on it, and spoke with a shaking voice. "You are now bound to this human because of this gift. I must assume you touched each other." He looked to his wife and questioned her, "Or, did you touch him first, Glenlillian?"

"No bond between us took place since Kim was the first to touch him, and he her," Glenlillian answered.

"What were you thinking, Kim?" her father demanded. "You should not have touched each other. And you certainly should not have accepted his gift."

"Luther, you are being ridiculous. We had to touch the man if we were to heal him," Kim's mother answered for her daughter.

His thunderous countenance told Glenlillian she had overstepped her bounds, and she did not speak again on the subject of Jahaziel.

Kim could not chance an explanation as to why she accepted Jahaziel's gift, and she began to cry. She could not tell them that before it was given to her, she had seen the beautiful ring in her dreams many times. She was in momentary shock—seeing the ring, and touching it, had rendered her speechless.

Her parents did not know of the insight Kim had acquired after tending an ill elf she had found crawling through the moors at

Phenloris. Her mind went quickly back to that moment and her strange encounter with the elf.

Chapter Three

It happened as she was gliding through the moors of Phenloris in order to be alone and, as her mother put it, "Contemplate her sins."

Kim finally sat. She took in a deep breath, and repeated her new litany to herself, "I will keep my mouth shut. I will keep my opinions to myself. I will not be boastful."

Again, "I will keep my mouth shut. I will keep my opinions to myself. I will not be boastful."

Before Kim could repeat her litany for the third time, she heard a soft moaning sound coming from a pile of boggy moss not far from where she sat.

She quickly rose in search of the sound, and could not believe what she had found. An adult elf was crawling across a pile of moss toward her, and she could clearly see he was in some sort of distress. When Kim lowered herself and knelt down, she realized he was very ill. A light touch upon his forehead revealed his burning fever.

"I don't know if you can understand me, but I cannot leave you here to die. I must go and fetch some water. Do not move from this spot. I will be back soon," Kim told the elf.

The elf grabbed Kim's arm in an attempt to stop her from leaving. She was now bonded to him, and he to her.

Kim quickly removed her apron and used it to wipe his hot, sweating face.

She spoke again to reassure him, "I promise I will be right

back. I was born with a strange gift that allows me to move from one place to another quickly. I will truly be back before you can blink your eyes."

Kim rose up, closed her eyes, and focused her mind to move beyond the here-and-now, and into that familiar place between. In one moment, she was back home. Quickly, without being seen, she entered the storeroom. With not much time to think, she collected a sack, and filled it with healing herbs, dried tree bark, dried vegetables, and her mother's specially prepared powdered broth mixture. She also found a blanket, her father's hooded guard's cloak that hung on a hook, and her mother's mixing stone. With the large and small clay pots placed in the sack as well, the whole bundle was heavier than Kim realized, and she nearly dropped it to the floor.

Holding tightly onto the sack, she peeked out of the storeroom door, and once again left her home to return to the spot where she had left the sickly elf.

Kim started a fire, and was glad the elf had fallen asleep. He did not awaken at her return, and Kim busied herself with mixing the additional herbs in the water she had collected on the way. She slowly stirred the mixture with a long piece of tree bark until it turned to a dark amber color. It was the last step in completing the recipe for wellness. This, she knew from her mother's teaching, would remove his fever and settle him into a long sleep.

"Sir, I need you to drink all of this broth. It will take away your fever and help you sleep," Kim told him.

She held the cup to his mouth, and helped him slowly sip the pleasant-tasting brew. As he slowly fell into a less-fitful sleep, Kim rolled her apron and gently placed it under his head, and then covered him with her father's cloak. Satisfied that he was warm, she built a frame for a make-shift tent out of large tree branches within her reach.

Then she covered the frame with the oversized blanket.

Kim kept the fire going until it was time for her to leave. As darkness began to descend, she knew returning home in all haste was imperative in order to avoid another lecture from her mother, and to save her poor ears that would surely burn from it.

Kim fell into a routine tending to the elf. On her way home each day, she would seek replacements for the herbs and bark she needed.

When Glenlillian questioned her activities, she simply said, "I found a special place where I can be alone and think about my faults. I understand it is time for me to grow up and be more responsible, Mother."

Glenlillian's tearful "yes" assured Kim her mother would not follow.

Finally, on the tenth day, the elf showed signs of recovery.

Kim's exhaustion showed on her face. She suspected that the dark circles under her eyes couldn't have been missed by the elf. But Kim did not let this stop her from going back and forth from her home to him each morning and evening until she was sure he was on the mend.

Feeling better than he had in days, the elf ate every bite of the food Kim prepared. Not only had he kept the food in his stomach, but he had asked Kim if there might be a bit more. A quiet conversation struck up between them. Kim told him about herself—more than he was willing to tell her about who he was, where he lived or what he was doing in their moors. However, he did tell her his name: Egwin.

"Egwin, I think you can start back to your home now, but please take your time and rest as often as you can. You may keep my father's cloak to protect you from the harsh weather about to befall us, but please send someone back here with it as soon as you are able. My father will wonder what has happened to the cloak, and he will not be happy that it is missing," she told the elf.

"I cannot leave until I pay you for your efforts and kindness, Kim," he said.

"Please. It is not necessary. I have done this of my own free will, and have not told a soul about any of this," Kim pleaded.

"You misunderstand me. It is our law, and I must abide by it."

"Truly, I do not wish anything. I cannot think of a thing that I need."

"Kimberlyn, fairy princess of the clan of Phenloris, stand and accept my gift!" the elf roared.

Kim quickly did as he said. The long song of the chanting prayer that issued from his lips was beautifully sung. When he finished, he told Kim he had given her the gift of insight. And, although it was an elfin trait alone, she deserved the gift for saving his life.

Kim's head had pounded. The instructions on how to control her gift were long and confusing. Egwin assured her she would be able to control everything in time, and with practice.

"I can walk with you until we reach the end of our moors, Egwin, if you do not mind my company a while longer," Kim said.

"Yes. That would be wonderful. Do you know any good stories? We elves love to tell tales, and even have contests to judge the best ones when we gather for our yearly goods exchange with other elf families," Egwin said.

"I happen to know many stories. Would you like to hear a true tale or a false tale?" she asked.

Egwin roared with laughter, and said, "Both."

Now it was Kim's turn to laugh, and she began her tale.

"First, I will tell you a true tale told to young fairies to ease their fear of stormy nights. My mother, Glenlillian, tells a tale about a family of crystal butterflies who come once every twelve hundred moons or so seeking food and shelter on their long migration through our lands."

Before Kim could continue her story, Egwin stopped her with his raised hand.

"Do you hear that?" he asked.

"No, I do not hear anything."

"There it is again."

"No, wait…I do hear something. It sounds like your name being called."

"Yes, it is. I must go now. I promise to take my time and have your cloak returned to you. We shall not see each other again." Egwin had to tell her that lie to keep Kim from looking for him. If she knew they would meet again, the future could change, and he could not risk a different outcome than what he already knew it to be.

Kim was confused and a little sad that Egwin had left so eagerly. He did not turn around to wave or smile as he disappeared down the hill and out of her sight.

Kim's mind snapped back to the present with her father's words. "Hush now. Stop your crying," Luther said. He hugged her to him. "We cannot change what has happened. Let us decide what to do now that this human knows of us."

The knock on the front door broke the sad mood, and Luther's command to enter had Glenlillian and Kim smiling at Huw's entrance. When he saw that Kim had been crying, he quickly embraced his betrothed while looking at Luther and Glenlillian for an answer.

However, Luther and Glenlillian quietly left their daughter and Huw alone to speak together, and to be with each other.

Huw knew better than to push Kim to speak when she was not ready to be forthcoming. He decided to talk about the one thing he knew she loved to hear him speak of. "I have finally finished the mesquite harp. Would you like to see it?" he asked her.

Kim's huge smile melted his heart, but her next words had him roaring with laughter.

"Does it smell as good as it sounds?" she asked.

So off they went, flying and laughing, to play the newest harp created by the only harp maker in the clan. And, it was a splendid thing to behold. The sound that emitted from the strings could send the listener into a blissful state. But, it also possessed fey magic when its strings were played in a secret order. This harp could move large, heavy objects, quiet storms and—unknown to Kim or her mother—could break spells.

The Black Knight was seated in a large chair made especially for his great size, waiting for his king to speak. He knew King Arnault was angry that he had not acquired the golden chalice. He kept his eyes focused on the fire burning in the hearth opposite the entrance of the newly conquered Castle Mead.

Located at the far edge and north of the dark forest, the castle lay well-hidden. Protected by winding hills, it had a large moat and high walls surrounding it. One full moon had come and gone since this knight and his large contingency of men had seized the castle, claiming it for his banished king.

Removing the servants of Castle Mead was the Black Knight's idea, forcing them to walk the long distance through the woods and into the dark forest. The banished king was in agreement. He secretly hoped those servants would be lost—forever wandering and seeking a way out.

Rumors spread that the forest was haunted. Some said it was guarded by strange creatures, and that those who dared to enter never returned. This certainly ensured there would be no witnesses left to tell of the siege. In his rage at not finding Castle Mead's King William in residence, or his attending knights, the king deliberately kicked over a pot of molten iron, knowing it would burn the outlying woods to the ground.

"You tell me you killed Jahaziel, captain of King Crawford's guard, yet you did not find the golden chalice? What were you thinking?" King Arnault screamed. "You should have tortured him until he broke, revealing its whereabouts. But no, you had to kill him. I should kill you myself for your stupidity, Gauwain."

"It is your prerogative, Sire." He spoke in a bored voice, knowing his king would do no such thing.

Stomping back and forth from one end of the great hall to the other, Arnault continued, "King Crawford is vulnerable without Jahaziel. I must take advantage of his mourning and make plans to force him into giving me the chalice."

He raised his hand in the air, and roared again, "I must have that chalice!"

After a long moment of silence he spoke once more. "Crawford's wife is about to give birth to their first-born child. Find his wife and bring her here. He will not allow harm to come to her. He will give me what I ask. Do not dare come back empty handed."

King Arnault's mind began to take him where he did not want to go—into the past. He began to recall the joust, his injuries, the long recovery, and his crushed hopes for a marriage match to Princess Joyce. He shook his head back and forth in an effort to blot out the missive he came upon just over one year ago. He put his fists to his eyes, rubbing them until the words faded. "It is with great pleasure that I, King Edward, announce the marriage of my daughter, Princess Joyce to Prince Crawford, on this twelfth day of August." He erased the rest of the missive from his mind.

Gauwain bowed to his king and set off on the journey, bound for Fitzhuwlyn Castle. He vowed, however, he would not let Arnault get his hands on Queen Joyce. He left in the dead of night to seek her out.

The journey was longer than he remembered, but this gave him the time he needed to plan the kidnapping and rescue. Making sure no one would see him taking her was one difficult part. Getting her on his horse quietly was the other.

The pack horse he brought with him was tired, so he stopped to rest it. He could not risk a fire, being so close to the castle keep, and settled himself at the well-shaded base of a large tree. He leaned his head back and fell asleep.

Gauwain dreamed of the siege, and people running and screaming in an effort to escape the great fire. His king's large hands were choking a woman into unconsciousness, and he was screaming at the king to stop.

Glenlillian, crystal fairy mother, slowly receded from the place where the Black Knight rested, and took great pains to not make a sound. Her intent was to search for her husband and seek his advice, but the pack horse and the black stallion belonging to Sir Gauwain smelled Glenlillian and began to prance and snort.

Gauwain quickly jumped to his feet from his sleeping position and, with sword in hand, turned to fight. Glenlillian stopped, frozen in motion, hiding among the plentiful Concordia flowers where all fairy babies were born. She held her breath, waiting for him to leave.

He took his time remounting his steed. When she was sure he was far enough away that she would not be seen, Glenlillian flew into a rage. Her words were heard only by the woodland creatures, causing them to scurry away from her in fear. Now, flying at her top speed, though not as fast as her daughter, she knew it would take her sometime to get home.

Her mind raced back to the day of the great fire, and the face of the laughing king. The people were running in different directions. They were so distressed at the prospect of being burned alive, they had no idea the fairy clan of Phenloris was doing the same. In her anger, Glenlillian had tried to remember the chant of crystal encasement—intent on encasing him on the spot as punishment—but she could not.

As she carefully glided through the woods, thoughts of her crowning celebration came to her. This rare gift, bestowed upon her as a tribute of valor by the fey King Cauluden, changed her rank from Glenlillian gold fairy to crystal fairy. This rare celebration had been bestowed upon one other fairy that she could recall in her long memory. Her name was Meirionwen, diamond fairy mother. She was Glenlillian's mother.

As she zigzagged through the dense woods, trying to avoid the large spikes of the green briers tightly wound through the copse of cedar trees, she smiled at the memory of her mother drinking from the beautiful diamond-encrusted, crystal chalice—the chanting and singing, the diamond tiara and silk cloak, the cheers, and laughter.

This brought to mind her ceremony celebrated in the same fashion. Like her mother before her, she now possessed the ability to encase anything or any creature in crystal forever. But this gift was to be used wisely. For, if it was not, the fairy possessing this power would be commanded to relinquish her power and title forever.

She slowly blinked her eyes, as they glistened with tears. Glenlillian was forever grateful, for she had yet to be called by an inquest to encase a fey or fairy. She knew well the finality of encasement. Her nightmares reminded her often.

How many times had she tried to forget the trauma inflicted upon her at such a young age?

She alone had been witness to the magical chant called forth by her mother onto herself. She had cried for days from the memory of seeing Meirionwen frozen in the crystal tomb. She had pounded on the large crystal until her hands were raw and bleeding, crying for her mother to come out. Weak and exhausted from sorrow, Glenlillian had lain on the floor of the cave, and had dreamed of the horrible fighting…

When the long battle at Bomey had ended badly, Meirionwen, covered with a fey cloak of invisibility, had continued searching for Merddlyn. Determined to state her argument for the tenth time, she would not show herself to humans. She had gotten in the way of the two men still in battle, and had been severely wounded. She had no idea Glenlillian had been following her, secretly hiding in the surrounding forest trees patiently waiting for her mother to stop her search for Merddlyn and head for home.

Alone, and in pain from the deep gash in her upper right leg that could not be healed quickly enough to save her life, she had managed to get to the secret cave, where she chanted the words of crystal encasement upon herself. Meirionwen, diamond fairy mother, stood frozen alongside Merddlyn, the greatest wizard of all time. They were forever hidden from man and greedy kings on the isolated Island of Bardfey.

It pained Glenlillian that she could not control her mind to forget her mother's death. She made a vow long ago to not speak to fey or fairy about that terrible day. Reliving the events of the battle always left her feeling depleted of energy and shaken. She stopped her sorrowful thoughts, snapped back to the present, and called upon the wind to assist her. She needed it at her back to help her get home quickly. She was intent on telling her husband of the Black Knight near King Crawford's keep.

Rising up to just above the tree line, she spoke the language of fairies. "I, Glenlillian, crystal fairy and mother, call upon the wind of the south to bring a gentle breeze. Assist me, assist me, will you please."

The wind did her bidding, and she reached her home in record time. Glenlillian flew inside with such force she knocked all her furnishings about. Clothes that had been stacked neatly on open shelves, as well as the dried flowers that had hung upside down from the ceiling, fell to the floor. But no one was home, and she could not recall where Luther or Kim had said they were going.

All Glenlillian could do now was calm down. It was not seemly for a crystal fairy mother to be so rattled. Picking up her favorite chair, she set it upright and sat down. Closing her eyes, she concentrated on slowing her breathing. With that accomplished, she focused on reaching her daughter and husband with her thoughts so they would come home.

Chapter Four

Kim spoke softly to her walking plant, Patience. In a conspiratorial voice, she said, "I need you to give this message to Sir Jahaziel for me, Patience. It is most important that I speak with him."

She placed the small handwritten message between her plant's long slender leaves. As Patience held it tightly to her, she made a soft sound only Kim could hear. Patience then lifted her leaves straight up—a gesture she often used to let Kim know she wanted to be picked up and held.

Kim continued to speak to her frightened plant, saying, "He will not hurt you, Patience, I promise."

Kim carefully glided out into the open meadow, and headed toward the castle in search of Sir Jahaziel. She was looking for a safe place to put Patience.

"I do not know why you are called a walking plant? You should be called a carry-me-plant," she said. Then, Kim smiled and patted her pot like a mother patting a baby, coaxing it to burp. She found the perfect spot to put Patience down. Then she spoke once more before leaving the area. "You understand what to do?"

Patience played with Kim's hair. All her leaves picked up strands of it—lifted them in the breeze—and then placed them in front of her face. Patience let go of the fine, long strands and touched Kim's face all over. Softly, Patience hugged Kim's entire head with every leaf and stem she possessed. Kim laughed at Patience's attempts to avoid being put down.

Aware Kim needed to leave the area before she was seen,

Patience let go of Kim's face and put her leaves and stems straight up. Stiff and without motion, Patience pretended to be an ordinary plant.

Kim took Patience through a small open window located on the west wall of Fitzhuwlyn Castle that faced the great hearth room. She set the plant upon a table she assumed was used for reading. It had one large candle upon it, and a very comfortable-looking chair next to it.

Kim gently touched Patience one more time for reassurance, then left. She glided quickly to the edge of the meadow, and waited for Jahaziel.

After long weeks of finding not one piece of information about the chalice, Jahaziel did not look forward to giving his report to the king.

Jahaziel sat in a chair next to a desk that was placed near a tiny window. He played absently with a plant's leaves, and mulled over what he would say to King Crawford. *The plant was obviously placed there to catch the morning sun,* he thought. Patience thoroughly enjoyed his attention.

With his concentration broken, Jahaziel tried very hard to focus on his seven-year-old sister, Siomara, who was screaming and running back and forth from hearth to serving hall. Her maid, Agnes, whose duties also included being second lady-in-waiting to the queen, raced after her. She was trying to comb the tangles from her overly long hair. Siomara was having none of it.

"Stop, stop, stop, let go of me, Agnes!" Siomara shouted.

"I will not let you walk around here looking like a wild she-wolf, Siomara. You will stand still and allow me to comb out this mess," Agnes replied. Before Siomara could escape Agnes' torture, she was yanked backward.

Jahaziel stood quickly and spoke in a harsh voice.

"Agnes, I will not tolerate your overbearing attitude toward my sister. If she does not want her hair ripped from her scalp, cut it off," Jahaziel admonished her.

Both women stared at the knight with their mouths open in shock. Agnes grabbed the only thing available.

Jahaziel ducked just in time to prevent the heavy wine goblet from knocking him senseless, and then burst out laughing as he watched the women quickly leave the room.

As he sat once again, his thoughts traveled back to the death of his parents six years ago and the kindness of Queen Joyce's father, King Edward. He had offered Jahaziel and his sister a permanent home after the tragic drowning of his wife, Queen Lenore; and the same offer was extended to those whom had attended to Queen Lenore on the journey back to her husband and home at Allenwood.

Jahaziel's parents were merchants from North /South land. Ever ready to inform Queen Lenore of the arrival of new goods and sewing materials to their trading post, they agreed to accompany the queen back to Allenwood, excited to visit with their newly knighted son. Whether it was insight or fate that his mother left his young sister with family, Jahaziel could not say. But, he was ever grateful that the fates had spared Siomara.

Upon their return, the river Aredoe had overflowed after a great storm, and the sheer force of the water had swept nearly everyone, including horses and wagon, into the sea. Jahaziel recalled Princess Joyce's eighteenth birthday was to be celebrated upon her mother's return. Instead, the king prepared for the funeral of his beautiful queen. Her body washed ashore among the debris of wagon wheels, boxes, clothing, and trees. King Edward could not bear to see Jahaziel return to his home, so he sent for his young sister when the roads were again, safe for travel.

A tiny tug on his shirtsleeve broke Jahaziel's train of thought. He glanced down, and expected to see what he thought might be a spider taking a walk. Instead, he was momentarily stunned, and could not believe his eyes. The plant was touching him. He blinked, and then leaned closer. An idea came to him, and he said quietly to the plant, "I do not suppose you belong to that cute little fairy named Kim, do you?"

Patience was so happy at his words she shook every part of herself in answer. Then she handed Jahaziel the message, relieved that she had done her duty to Kim. While Jahaziel read Kim's message, Patience stroked his hand to let him know she understood. With the note still in his hands, Jahaziel stared at the fireplace that was set to burn off the morning chill before the castle jumped into activity. He slowly rose, read the message again, and then left the hall. Patience was stunned that he did not take her with him.

Oh, oh, oh, what am I to do now? she wondered. Before she could decide to climb down off the table to escape outside, she heard footsteps.

Queen Joyce spoke to the pretty little plant, and tried to figure out who had given her such a sweet gift. "You will be much happier in my rooms than downstairs. I fear you would be knocked off my reading table when the servants come to clean. Some of them are quite clumsy, and my sleeping room window is much larger than the reading window downstairs," she said to Patience.

Queen Joyce patted the plant's pot for reassurance, and then returned downstairs to tackle the duties of the day. Poor Patience was so upset that she allowed all her stems and leaves to droop down over the rim of her pot and onto the table. She whimpered to herself, and knew she could not get out of this room without help. So she fell asleep with the early morning sun shining on her forlorn, sad self.

Kim was happy to see Jahaziel riding toward her. She

smiled brightly, and moved quickly from her hiding spot to meet him halfway. Just inches from his face, she could see the dark look he was giving her.

Kim was confused by the dark mood, and decided to give him back the same attitude. She moved slightly backward, put a scowl on her face and, with her hands on her hips, said, "None of this is my fault. And you can stop looking at me like that. Do you hear me, Sir Jahaziel?"

His soft chuckle stopped the rest of her words. Jahaziel tugged at Kim's dress, and slowly brought her closer to his face again.

"Your message only mentioned trouble was coming. Explain what you meant by 'trouble coming,'" Jahaziel said.

She did not take her eyes from Jahaziel, and could not seem to find her words either. All she did was stare at him and smile. Kim knew that Jahaziel was attracted to her, and she to him. *What kind of a friendship could we have, fairy and knight?* Kim wondered.

He tugged lightly on her dress again, and waited for her answer.

Kim snapped out of her thoughts, and slowly began her long tale of the fire in the forest at Castle Mead.

"I hold you to secrecy, Sir Jahaziel. Do you agree to this?"

"Yes, of course, Kim."

"Our clan has existed since before man could count what he perceives as time. Before the occupation of men in our area, and the building of a large structure began, we fairies lived in the forest we call Phenloris. Our homes were well-hidden, and protected by its denseness, and it contained within its borders many healing plants," she told him.

"I was sent to a sister clan north of Phenloris by my mother to collect and trade vessels, herbs, and recipes. That was just before the fire. I was taken by surprise when my father came to collect me with a large contingent of fey guards accompanying him. What he told me was shocking, and I cried for hours from the telling, Jahaziel. My father is a wise fey King and…"

"Your father is a King?" Jahaziel interrupted.

"Well, yes."

"Does that mean you are a princess?" he asked her with a smile.

"Stop interrupting me. I will forget my train of thought," Kim said, laughing.

"The man known to you as King William, according to my father's observations, had a structure built that he referred to as Castle Mead. One afternoon, during a practice with his guards, my father observed many occupants of the castle leaving on horses, including King William. And they had not returned. Others came instead and arguments ensued.

"A very tall, well-muscled man, dressed completely in black, was arguing with another man just outside the north end of our forest. He addressed this man as 'Sire.' My father could see the tall man was not happy hearing the words of the other man, because he was shaking his head no, over and over again. In a fit of rage, the angry man kicked over a pot of hot liquid. A great fire leapt, and spread quickly.

"We were all in shock. The poor serving people of Castle Mead were screaming and running everywhere. My father had little time to gather up the clan and move to safety. We wandered for many days looking for a new home. Our hope was that we would be able to return to Phenloris once the forest heals itself with time and fairy care.

"My father returned to the edge of the meadow near our forest. Hidden, he observed the tall man and angry man once again in a heated argument.

"My father heard the angry man giving orders to the tall man to kill the servants. There was more arguing, and then the angry man nodded his head. The tall man pushed the servants into the west end of our forest, and through an area we ourselves do not go."

Kim looked down for a moment. She hoped that Jahaziel would not detect her lie of not going into the dark forest. She had gone into that forest many times. "This is a dark and dangerous place, and humans should not be there," she said.

"When I thought I could bear no more of this telling, my father went on with his story. This angry man was obsessed with acquiring a treasured chalice that belongs to our clan. This chalice is made of the purest gold, encrusted with jewels. Folded within the gold of its forging are properties of the magic of magic.

"Also, a guinea cava told me about a strange man asking questions of the people who live near your castle. He was inquiring as to the whereabouts of a lost article. LuLu Piggy said the people refused to answer, and went about their business. From Lulu's description of this man—his black clothing—I suspect it to be the man my father spoke of," she concluded.

Jahaziel smiled at the thought of Kim speaking to the guinea pig. Then he said, "You have just confirmed what I told you when we first met. Do you remember?"

"Yes," Kim answered. "However, I was not permitted to speak on the matter. I have yet to be given permission, Jahaziel. And I will more than likely get into trouble if my father finds out."

"Kim, the man you call the angry man is a king also. His name is Arnault, and he is not a good man or a good king. I am truly sorry that your people suffered at his hands. He had no cause to set that fire, Kim. I am much clearer in my understanding of how his twisted mind formed the idea to burn the forest near

Fitzhulyn Castle. I heard he became enraged when his efforts were thwarted. The man in black is called Sir Gauwain. Now I understand why he wants this chalice. But, I have a question still unanswered. Who told King Arnault that King Crawford has this chalice?"

"I do not know," Kim replied.

"King Crawford asked me why I thought fairies had suddenly showed themselves in the area of our keep. I realize now that I am the answer to his question. I am the reason you have shown yourselves," Jahaziel said.

"Yes. That is true," Kim replied. "However, this Arnault was told of our chalice before I found you, and things were already set into motion. Finding fairies would not have been very much later."

"Perhaps," Jahaziel replied. He thought a moment, and spoke again. "Kim. Is it possible that a fey guard or fairy told Arnault of your chalice?"

"I cannot say positively, no," Kim answered. "We are all who we are. But the punishment for this fey or fairy would be unspeakable."

"I need to speak with your father, Kim."

"I cannot let you come to my home. My father would have a fit if he saw you. And, I would be punished for my carelessness."

"Was saving my life careless?"

"I did not mean it that way, Sir Jahaziel. However, my father would say so." Kim lowered her head in shame at her words, and held her hands together in frustration.

Jahaziel continued his speech, and every word he spoke he said with great care.

"I need to know more about Castle Mead's takeover. King William is a good friend, and second cousin to King Crawford's wife. He had not been aware that King William was on a pilgrimage. Then the queen realized her forgetfulness and told her husband where King William had gone, and that he had left a request not to be disturbed. I am glad that his knights had been off honoring contracts from other lords in the area. There would have been much loss of life had all been in residence.

"I am concerned about the servants still lost in that strange forest. They must be recovered and sent to King Crawford. Word must also be sent to King William and his knights. The Black Knight must be questioned, and King Arnault needs to be dealt with as well.

"I cannot tend to all this alone. I need help. Perhaps you can speak to the piggy again and get more information. I have been commissioned by King Crawford to take care of this. I will not involve all my men unless it is absolutely necessary. Most importantly, your clan must not let the chalice fall into the hands of Arnault."

Kim's head pounded from worry, and her stomach began to ache. She nodded her agreement, and Jahaziel followed Kim to her home.

Jahaziel stopped his horse at Kim's fear-filled voice.

"Where is Patience?" she asked.

"Who is Patience?"

"The plant," she stammered. "The plant on the table that gave you my message!" she shouted.

"Stop shouting at me, Kim. I did not think to bring that strange plant with me. You did not write me to bring it."

"No, no, no," she chanted on and on. "I cannot believe I lost my favorite walking plant. Hope and Temperance will not understand. And they cannot sleep if Patience is not there with them.

I am in so much trouble. I might as well drown myself in a lake."

When she finally stopped talking, Jahaziel questioned her. "Your plants walk?" He held up his hand quickly in an attempt to stop her words, and then continued, "Never mind—do not tell me more. I have had enough talk, and I have no intention of going back to fetch your plant."

He closed his eyes, and sighed. Blessed quiet engulfed them and only the sound of the distant birds could be heard singing their sweet songs of happiness.

Jahaziel opened his eyes when he heard Kim crying softly to herself. He moved ahead, grabbed her around her waist, and gently brought her to his shoulder, turning her as he did so. With her face up against his shirt, she cried all the harder. He gently patted her back, and hoped her mother would not see such an awful display.

When her hiccups told him she was finished with her tears, he spoke softly to her, "Kim, sweetie, stop your crying now. I did not mean to shout at you. I swear by all that is holy, you do try my patience. Are not fairies calmly unshakeable, quietly serene, patiently meditative, hopeful beyond measure, uniquely secretive?"

He stopped his litany when he heard her giggle. "That is much better. I do not like seeing women cry. And it distresses me to think that I have caused your tears," he said.

Kim stayed at Jahaziel's shoulder and fell asleep. He held her gently, and smiled, and wondered what the king would think if he saw them like this. Then he frowned, and wondered what Kim's father would think if he saw them like this.

His horse slowed to a stop when Kim told him they were at her home. Glenlillian rushed out to meet Kim, and stopped immediately when she saw Jahaziel. In rushed words, she said, "Why have you brought Sir Jahaziel here? Are you deliberately trying to provoke your father? He will have a fit if he sees him.

Have you been crying, Sweetling?”

Glenlillian changed her direction of thought so fast Jahaziel blinked in surprise. Before Kim could respond, she started crying again. Glenlillian held her daughter—cooing soothing nonsense words. Jahaziel looked to the heavens for patience.

Coming around from behind the knight, Kim’s father roared. “What have you done to my daughter?”

Chapter Five

Queen Joyce decided to take her mind off her worries and go for a walk. With her new plant in her arms, she headed for her garden—for the sun was shining and a warm, soft breeze was blowing.

Her arguments with Agnes were pointless and, as much as she disliked bringing her troubles about servants to her husband, she knew there was no choice in this matter. Agnes had to go. And her husband was the only person who could command such a decision.

She was not a cruel woman, however, and took it upon herself to search—with the aid of two servants—for an abandoned cottage where Agnes could live comfortably. With that sad task accomplished, and in her gentle manner, she would ask her husband to allow the cottage to be filled with all the things necessary for living—down to lighting a fire in the hearth.

She looked about her, and smiled at the memory of her husband working secretly in the night to have the garden ready as a surprise. He had done all the work himself. He had wanted his wife to be able to see the colorful beauty from their sleeping room window. He had been so happy when she told him they were going to have a baby that he had decided then and there to create this garden with as much regal splendor as possible for his wife and child to enjoy for many years to come.

She placed her plant down in a softly shaded area, and knelt down to water it. Being so heavy with child, she had difficulty standing back up. Then she heard a deep, male voice behind her.

"May I assist you my lady?"

She assumed it was one of the many knights roaming the castle and grounds, so she said, "Yes," and stood with his assistance. Then, in one quick motion, he lifted her up and onto a horse.

The Black Knight held on tightly to the queen, and spoke in rushed words and whispered, "Your Majesty, you must not scream for help. You are in grave danger from a king I serve who wishes to harm you. He has demanded I bring you to him, but I will take you to a safe place where he will not find you. There is no time for me to explain. We must leave in all haste before anyone sees us. If I must, I will kill anyone who comes to your aid. He then kicked his horse into a run, and whisked the queen away from her home and safety without being seen.

Hours later, the knight stopped to rest his horses, and the queen pleaded for him to let her walk a bit.

"If you promise me you will not try to run off, I will let you walk among those flowers over there," he said, pointing.

"Look at me, sir knight. I could not run if my life depended on it."

Clearly embarrassed, Gauwain simply smiled.

"I do see your point, Your Majesty. My name is Gauwain."

"Sir Gauwain, I am Joyce."

Sir Gauwain reached up and gently lowered her to the ground. To ease her concerns, he struck up a conversation with her.

"How much more time do you have before the birthing of your child?" he asked.

They walked together toward the flowery meadow, and

Joyce spoke in a breathless voice.

"Not long now. Our midwife suspects less than a month. I hear talk among the servants who have children that a woman always knows when her time comes near. I must confess I do not have such insight. This is our first child, and I am new to my pending motherhood. May we sit a moment, Sir Gauwain? I grow tired."

"Certainly."

They sat down at the base of a large willow tree that provided ample shade, and continued their conversation. Moments later, the queen fell asleep, curled up near the base of the tree.

Gauwain carefully lifted Joyce into his arms and leaned against the tree. He hugged her gently to him, and made the decision to not speak of the war that was about to begin.

The long, two-day journey zigzagging away from castles Mead and Fitzhuwlyn was slow and difficult. Queen Joyce struggled to remain calm. She had no appetite, and ate very little of the food that was offered to her.

Sir Gauwain finally relaxed at the sight of the well-hidden structure. It was a half-built, abandoned castle he had found and made ready for himself when he no longer had contract to serve King Arnault. He handed Queen Joyce over to the two loyal servants who were in residence, and gave the order to lock her in the upper room of his chamber until he returned with some provisions. He commanded this be done for her safety. If she were to escape, she might wander and get lost.

Queen Joyce slept for several hours, barely waking for food and drink. While a servant cleaned the room and chatted with her to keep up her strength for the sake of the baby, she ate only a small portion of the fare.

She wondered what was taking her husband so long to find her. Surely, someone may have witnessed her being taken, and must be looking for her. Perhaps they have just now sounded an alarm. They knew she should not be perched upon a horse in her condition, so they would check wagons and carts coming and going.

Where was Sir Jahaziel? And where were the knights under his command? Her head started pounding, and her back began to ache. She gave in to her exhaustion, and slept again. In her dreams she saw a sparkling light coming to her rescue.

Jahaziel's head started pounding—not because of Kim or Glenlillian—but from Kim's father's continued shouting. When he finally stopped his tirade, Jahaziel deliberately enunciated his words so no mistake would be made as to his meaning.

"I have come here to warn you of the possibility of a traitor lurking within your own clan. I will not, however, take your abusive conduct toward me or your daughter lightly. Make no mistake, Luther, once I leave, I will not offer my assistance or ask for yours again. Do you get my meaning, sir?"

Taken aback by Jahaziel's strong words, Lutherian made a wise decision, and did not speak again. Instead he went into his home and slammed the door shut. Jahaziel turned his horse and nudged him to run, and headed in all haste toward Fitzhuwlyn Castle.

Jahaziel's last thought was that he hoped Luther would not turn him into a frog when his back was turned.

Kim and Glenlillian hovered motionless. They were unable to speak—shocked at what they had just witnessed. Then mother and daughter fell to the ground in hysterical laughter. Never had they seen Luther ever struck speechless. Nay, it was going to be a memory in the history of Clan Phenloris for years to come.

Luther knew his wife was right. He frowned and mumbled to himself, but he did not have the stomach to tell her this. And his pride would not let him. It was inevitable that they would help Sir Jahaziel, but showing themselves to the wandering servants from Castle Mead was another thing altogether.

Instead, his wife offered the solution to him by declaring Gilthew Law.

This ancient declaration gave a fey or fairy the right to command a gathering of the entire fairy clan for a vote. It also gave a fairy the power to be heard without interruption.

The only problem was finding the traitor before the gathering. He knew if Jahaziel's assumptions were correct and the vote to assist Jahaziel went in his favor, the traitor would go to King Arnault to warn him of an impending attack.

Then, he thought like a head fey guard and king. He surmised that half the guard could go with Jahaziel, and the other half into the dark, Haunted Forest.

All who were assembled waited for Glenlillian to begin speaking. She had called upon the wind to send her message of Gilthew to all her clan. Under a canopy of dense trees, the assembled fairies spoke to each other in low voices, waiting for the uninterrupted speech to begin.

Before speaking, Glenlillian dispatched a warning to Luther and Kim by way of a guinea pig messenger to keep a watchful eye out for suspicious behavior from any fey or fairy.

She said a quick prayer that Jahaziel would already be with his king, informing him he must retake Castle Mead for King William.

There was little time between here and there to root out the traitor she was sure was among the assembled clan.

Malcolm Fey Crier came forward, and in a loud voice announced Gilthew had been proclaimed. "Glenlillian crystal fairy mother now has the right of speech. All will listen. All will remain quiet. All will heed our law," he said, as he nodded his head to Glenlillian.

She floated forward and began, saying, "A human named Sir Jahaziel, knight and captain of King Crawford's Guard, has been exposed to our existence. He has made a formal claim to your king for assistance. He speaks of the humans wandering the dark forest who were forced from their homes when the great fire burned and forced all to flee. We had our own homes destroyed in the process. We suffered as much as these humans and we continue to be devastated by this loss.

"We have found a new home here in the forest that outlies Fitzhuwlyn Castle, property and keep. And, we have not been disturbed. The people who fled as we did still wander lost in the dark forest. There is no way out for them, and they will eventually die from starvation and illness. I claim voting rights to show ourselves to them and assist in all ways needed. A nay or yea by show of hands I ask of all assembled."

Glenlillian was so relieved at the show of hands to assist she finally began to relax. Her back was so stiff it started aching, and her hands shook at the thought all would vote against her.

The count was finally finished, and the decision to help was made. Luther watched the assembled fairies from the back of the crowd, and noticed movement. He nodded to his second-in-command. Broadwayne followed the fey guard sneaking out before assembly prayer was finished. The traitor was found.

"Broadwayne, throw him in the guard hut and keep watch he does not escape. When this mess is cleared up, I will return to deal with him later, and decide on his punishment."

"Yes, King Lutherian, I will see to it."

He shook his head as he walked to gather up those willing to assist in the rescue of King William's people.

He mumbled, "My head pounds at the thought of Jahaziel being correct in his assumptions of a traitor among us."

Chapter Six

King Crawford's roar of anguish was heard outside in the courtyard. He could not find his wife, and his heart pounded with pain and worry. He called to his guards while he ran, and barked orders to his knights to gather weapons and provisions.

A holler from the north-tower wall brought his attention to the meadow below the castle. Jahaziel was coming fast, and the king hoped—nay prayed—that Jahaziel knew where his wife was.

Jahaziel stopped his horse quickly, and caused dust to rise high around him. The king barked questions at him so fast he could not understand the man.

Not again, he thought. *What is it with all this yelling? Can they not just speak in normal voice and attitude?* His head started pounding again, and he dismounted slowly, waiting for his king to finish. When the King's words began to register, Jahaziel, himself, flew into a rage at what he was being told.

Queen Joyce was stunned to see that the black knight had returned to his home, and now knelt before her to formally pledge himself as her personal knight and additional protector. She nearly burst into tears.

The look on his face showed his sincerity.

"Thank you, Sir Gauwain. I accept your pledge. Please sit down and rest yourself."

"Thank you." He sat and waited for permission to speak again.

At her nod, he explained, "I do not know if you have heard of my reputation, Your Majesty. But I am not as heartless as people have been told. It has been my great misfortune to be commanded to serve King Arnault. Had I known his intent was to capture Castle Mead and kill King William, I would not have answered his command. It was King William himself who sent me to Arnault. My only sin was obedience. I harmed no one in the onslaught, and I convinced King Arnault to force the servants into the dark forest. He would have preferred to kill them all, so I had no choice. As far as you are concerned, my only desire is to keep you safe. This is the only place I could think to bring you. King Arnault will hear I have taken you. He will be satisfied that we are on our way to him. This will give your husband time to recapture Castle Mead."

Her composure finally broke, and Queen Joyce began to cry. Sir Gauwain scooped her up into his arms again, and held her until she fell into an exhausted asleep.

He shook his head slightly, and chastised himself. *I should not have mentioned the battle*, he thought to himself. He placed her gently down upon the well-prepared bed. He then covered her, and quickly headed out. He put on his armor and, with a scowl on his face, gained his horse and headed in the direction of Castle Mead.

The journey back to Castle Mead gave Gauwain the time he needed to form a plan. He knew that if he came upon King Crawford's knights they would kill him before he could explain himself, and tell them where to find their queen.

He worried she would go into labor from the long journey, and from being upset. He was glad he had left instructions with his servants to keep on their guard, and to attend the young, expectant queen.

She did not look well to him when he left, and he said a

quick prayer that she would still have a few days left before the birthing. Queen Joyce may have forgiven him for his folly, but King Crawford would not give him the chance. What Gauwain needed was a liaison to take a message to King Crawford before he arrived. *But whom?* he wondered.

Gauwain stopped his horse, turned around, and headed toward Polnairs Retreat, where he hoped King William was still on pilgrimage. Because of his request for isolation so he could have private prayer, and meditation, the king would not have been aware of the circumstance that had taken place in the month he had been gone from his home.

With time already wasted heading for Castle Mead, Sir Gauwain gave his horse the signal to move at top speed. He didn't stop until he reached the retreat, nearly killing his horse in the process. When he finally approached, Gauwain slowed his horse to a trot.

The servants of the retreat spotted the horseman some distance away, and ran toward him. Gauwain barked orders for someone to tend his exhausted horse as he jumped from the saddle.

"I am Sir Gauwain. Who can take me to King William?"

At first they refused, but quickly changed their minds when they saw him take his sword from its loop.

An elderly servant rushed forward and introduced himself, saying, "I am Bartholomew, and I can take you to the king."

Bartholomew was an elderly gentleman, and Gauwain had difficulty in getting him to move forward more quickly. Retreat servants did not run. Servant Bartholomew kept stumbling, and actually fell forward once. If it had not been for the knight grabbing him and pulling him upright, he would have fallen and surely harmed himself.

At their entrance to the retreat house of Polnairs, Gauwain started yelling, "King William, I must speak with you. It is a matter of grave importance!"

"Please. Stop yelling, Sir Gauwain, he cannot hear you. The king is here just beyond this door," Bartholomew said.

Bartholomew rushed ahead of the knight, opened wide the heavy door, then stepped aside. When Gauwain rushed through, he slammed the door shut behind him.

Sir Gauwain knelt before his former king and friend, and hoped that he made sense with everything he was telling the king. They had no time for him to repeat himself. Precious moments had already been wasted while Gauwain was deciding to come here for King William's assistance.

"I was in great error, Gauwain, when I gave you command to serve Arnault. I knew he was ruthless and could be cruel at times, but I had no choice in the matter. I had wished to exchange you for my wife's young cousin who was serving Arnault as page. I had no reservations that you could take care of yourself, and that Arnault would jump at the chance to have you for one year. Young Alex was witness to Arnault's abusive nature on more than one occasion, and I could not in all good conscience leave the boy there.

"Had I not made the exchange, things would be very different now. Do not berate yourself Gauwain. Queen Joyce is safe because of you. Come, let us go in haste to Crawford together and right this wrong."

When the last of the fairies had left the clearing after their unanimous decision to enter the dark forest to retrieve the lost people, Glenlillian spoke quietly to her husband. "I believe you should send a guard to Jahaziel and let him know those chosen to assist him are ready to leave for the dark forest near Castle Mead."

"I have already dispatched Cassiarian. He is quick of flight, and was told to be careful—to not allow himself to be seen by others," Luther replied.

"It will be strange to return to Phenloris after being away for so long. Do you not think, Lutherian?"

"Yes, my sweet. It will be difficult for all of us."

At that same moment, Kim began to get flashes of a place beyond the forests and meadows. She did not recognize any of it, but she knew something was wrong.

Her instincts to be cautious were never without merit. She told her mother she was in need of a bit of air, then followed her instincts and moved with great speed to the place of her visions.

Kim stopped to rest a moment, her breaths coming fast while she focused on her surroundings. She had covered many miles since she had left, so she decided to walk for a bit to regain her strength. She looked around, and found kiwis hanging on large vines that were starting to recede as the sun began its decent.

She found the largest one, and plucked it off and munched while she walked. It felt so good to walk that she decided to take a run. She bent down near a small stream to wash her hands. Then she stood and took off running. Kim laughed out loud from the sheer pleasure of it, and ran until her lungs could no longer catch breath.

The insight then took hold of her, and she focused on what she saw. She closed her eyes, and then willed herself to go to that place. She rose up above the trees, and gathered the energy that she was saving. In one fairy moment she was there.

She hovered until her dizziness passed, then slowly lowered herself to the ground. Darkness had fallen, and Kim gently touched the tips of her wings to create a soft sparkling glow around her. She could see a little better, so she cleared her head and looked around. That was when she heard the moaning sounds. It was a woman, and she sounded as if she were in a great deal of pain.

She followed the sound, which led Kim to the small, half-constructed castle. She rose high up to a parapet and peeked into a long, narrow opening used for shooting out arrows. A young woman paced back and forth from door to fireplace, and held onto her back, whimpering softly. Kim squeezed herself through the tiny window, tearing her dress at the shoulder as she went. She fell to the floor with a loud thud. Then she quickly gained her feet, and slowly floated up, facing the woman.

Queen Joyce stood still and did not dare breathe. The queen quickly searched her mind. She tried to recall childhood stories about fairies, and wondered if this was such a creature? Joyce was so shocked by the possibility, all she could do was smile.

Kim smiled back, and spoke, saying, "My name is Kim, and I heard your distress. May I assist you in whatever way you may need?"

Joyce bent over slightly to relieve her back pain, and whispered, "Can you birth a baby?"

"Excuse me. Did you say you can mirth and pay me?"

"No. Can you birth-a-ba-by?" Joyce said, enunciating every syllable.

"No way on all of this earth, my family, your family, every creature and then some!" Kim shouted.

"Then leave here, and let me be."

Joyce spoke so despondently, Kim could only smile. She asked the queen if she was alone, then went in search of the servants she was told were below stairs. After their initial shock at hearing a fairy giving orders, they rushed to do her bidding.

Satisfied that she had everything she needed to assist the beautiful woman in her laboring, Kim asked her what her name was.

"I am Joyce, Queen, and wife of King Crawford."

Kim's eyes opened wide with surprise and concern.

The queen continued, "I was abducted by the one called the Black Knight, and brought here by a rare twist of fate for my own protection." The queen bent over again from the pain, and took quick, short breaths. "I am sorry, but this baby comes now. Could you please fetch Mrs. Jones, Kim? I am in need of her help."

"Yes, of course. But I must also seek further assistance."

Kim decided to send for Sir Jahaziel. *How long does it take for human babies to come?* she wondered. She could think of no answer. She closed her eyes and mind to all around her and willed an eagle to come. At the sound of his flapping wings, Kim quickly went to the little window and gave the hovering bird Jahaziel's ring. She spoke to it in her ancient language, then waved her hand for it to go quickly. The large bird flew away to do Kim's bidding.

With her pains gone for the moment, Queen Joyce asked Kim what she was doing.

"I was calling for help."

"How can this be done?"

"I cannot explain it to you, but you must trust me."

"At his point, I do not know who I can trust. It is all so confusing to me. Just yesterday I was placing the most beautiful potted plant in my garden to have a little sun, and now I am here—told it is for my own safety. I believe Sir Gauwain, but I am sure he has not told me everything."

Queen Joyce sat on the only stool in the room, intent on taking the strain off her back. "Do you know of this king called Arnault, Kim?"

"My father mentioned him, but I do not know the man."

Kim put a cloth in the water basin, wrung it out and started gently wiping the queen's face. Queen Joyce smiled at Kim's ministrations, and wondered if all fairies were like her. She was becoming more comfortable, so Joyce asked Kim about her family—where she lived, her age, and how did she get her hair to curl like that. Kim smiled as she touched her recently curled hair, and only answered the last question.

"My mother made these wonderful little sticks cut from a willow branch. After wetting my hair, she wound strands of it around the sticks, and tied them with morning glory vine. After my hair dried, she removed the sticks—and now I have these curls."

The queen smiled, and asked, "Do you think you could arrange my hair in such a manner when I am returned home?"

"Oh, yes. It would be my pleasure, Your Majesty."

"Please, Kim, call me Joyce. We are friends now."

"Joyce, the plant you speak of is my walking plant. Her name is Patience, and she was a gift from my mother. She is a very kind and attentive plant, and has two sisters. Hope and Temperance will be so very happy to know she is safe and well. I was frantic thinking I had lost her."

"Kim, I am sorry. I did not know this. I will return Patience to you when I am home once again. But, do all your plants walk?"

"No, only the lesson plants do. They teach young fairies lessons of responsibility, and they build character." When she realized Joyce did not understand, she continued, "For example, Patience teaches me how to be patient. She is very difficult to care for and requires a lot of attention. Hope teaches me how to be hopeful. She does not show me her rare blooms that my mother speaks of. My hope is that one day she will find me worthy. Temperance teaches me how to use moderation in all things. I cannot rush her when it is her feeding time because her roots are shorter than the others. Therefore, I must feed her more often than I do Patience and Hope. I am relieved to know Patience is well-taken-care-of. She is not afraid of the dark, so you need not worry over that."

As the queen's labor pains began, then ended, once again, Kim and Joyce continued to speak awhile longer, thankful for the much-needed break.

In the distance, the sound of thunder could be heard, and the queen thought it was a fitting sign to announce the birth of her child.

Chapter Seven

The war began and ended quickly once King Crawford had gained entry to Castle Mead. The fighting was down to a few skirmishes, and the battle would become a thing of legend.

To the soldiers walking outside Castle Mead's gates, King Crawford's large army of men, on horseback and on foot, had seemed to come from out of nowhere. The sound of their thundering approach had been a complete surprise. Stationed as lookouts, they had not been prepared for such a battle.

"Jahaziel!" King Crawford hollered as they seemed to fly down the hill toward Castle Mead. "I need you to gain entry and find Arnault. He must be questioned. Do not kill the man. I know it is your desire to do so."

Jahaziel nodded his agreement, and he, along with King Crawford, the fey guards, and the king's army, had surged forward, and had quickly set upon the soldiers pouring out from every entryway to the castle. By command from Arnault, his soldiers were to fight to the death.

Shouting men had prepared to meet in the clashing of swords, horses, fire and death as they had run toward one another in blinding fury.

Inside, Arnault ran around gathering anything he could find of value. Into a large sack he shoved jewelry, gold coins, goblets of silver, and clothing. A shout from his personal guard, Royce, stopped his movements, and he turned toward the entryway.

"King Arnault, Jahaziel approaches quickly. Our men are outnumbered and most of the exits are blocked by King Crawford's soldiers," Royce warned.

"Kill him, you idiot. Stop him. I must escape and seek out Gauwain. Since he has not yet returned with Crawford's wife, I must assume he has had a change of heart, and has taken her elsewhere. I will kill him for disobeying me," King Arnault replied.

The arrow came from nowhere, and hit Royce in the leg. He fell to the ground, and was immediately grabbed by the two soldiers flanking Jahaziel.

The sack Arnault held fell to the ground as he was lifted off his feet. Jahaziel had his hand securely around Arnault's neck, and the king made choking sounds as he tried to kick the knight's legs out from under him. Jahaziel then threw the king across the room, where he hit a wall and fell to the floor, unconscious.

Jahaziel picked him up, tied him to a chair, and waited for King Crawford.

In his fury, King Crawford quickly re-captured Castle Mead for King William.

Unprepared for such a large contingency of soldiers, knights, and a surprisingly large group of fey guards, King Arnault, now awake and filled with rage reluctantly conceded his defeat. King Crawford slapped Arnault a few times yelling his demand that he tell them where Queen Joyce was being held.

"You think I will tell you, Crawford. You are an idiot. I can hold my tongue. Sir Gauwain is at this very moment taking her to a secret place by my order. If he does not hear from me soon, he will do as I commanded, and he will kill her. He is loyal to me—and me alone," King Arnault said, sneering.

It was his last lie before Crawford punched him so hard he fell to the floor, still tied to the chair, unconscious once again.

Jahaziel realized they would not get answers from Arnault, so they locked him in the dungeon below the large wine and storage cellar.

"My question is the whereabouts of my wife and Sir Gauwain," King Crawford spoke, his voice strained from so much yelling. "I have questioned the few servants here, and we know Arnault is not talking. What say you, Jahaziel?"

"I do not know, sire," Jahaziel answered. "I wish I did. But I have no idea."

"I understand that some of the fairy menfolk have gone into the dark forest to retrieve William's people? Is this true?"

"Yes, Sire, and I have great faith that they will recover everyone," Jahaziel answered again.

"I believe I am still in somewhat of a shock seeing fey guards in the flesh," King Crawford said. "You should have warned me of their arrival, Jahaziel. It would have prevented what I am sure was a surprised look on my face.

They demonstrated great skill as knights of so short stature—compact, yet strong, are these creatures of the fairy race. This clan, called Phenloris, is a grand and wondrous clan. I am honored and forever grateful for their assistance. I must remember to thank their king. Luther, you say, Jahaziel?"

Before Jahaziel could answer, several servants came into King William's large study and put food and water on a wooden table. Crawford and Jahaziel, along with several of his knights and two royal guards, had come inside to regroup and sit awhile to think on the matter of Queen Joyce. No one spoke while they ate. All kept their own counsel.

"I need wine," King Crawford hollered, breaking the silence. A servant within earshot ran in, bowed, and ran back out in all haste to do the king's bidding. This servant was so relieved to see King Crawford's approach he forgot himself. Close to tears, he ran to the king, and grabbed him in a great bear hug. Just as quickly, he jumped back with profound apologies stammering from his lips. To his utter amazement, King Crawford grabbed him back, hugged him, and slapped him on his back. The king then said, "I am happy to see you again, John."

After the wine was served to everyone, John went to Sir Jahaziel. With eyes wide open with surprise, he told him a fairy was in the entrance hall waiting to speak to him.

Jahaziel smiled a warm smile at the approach of Glenlillian.

"We are all happy for the assistance of King Crawford's knights," Glenlillian said to Jahaziel. "The journey into the dark forest will be a challenge. I believe the people will be more at ease once they see the knights, as it will lessen their shock of seeing fey guards. I also came to tell you very few fairies or feys voted against you, Jahaziel. And I was glad they let their hearts lead them to do the right thing. However, there is one more matter I wish to discuss. It is not necessary to hide Kim from her father. He is no longer angry that she brought you to our home. He wishes to apologize for his outburst. Anyway, I could use her assistance when we go into the dark forest. She knows her way around this strange place. Though, I must confess, I do not know how, for the life of me, this has come to be. She has grown up so fast I cannot keep up with her abilities."

She ended her words, and waited for Jahaziel to answer.

He looked confused, remembering Kim's words that the fairies did not enter the dark, strange woods. He realized her lie, and hoped that worry would not come through his voice as he said to Kim's mother, "I do not have Kim here with me, Glenlillian. How long has she been missing?"

Glenlillian looked stunned, and Jahaziel's words did not seem to register immediately. Then she closed her eyes, breathed in and out, and said, "Over half of this day now, and it will be dark soon."

Jahaziel did not miss the sadness and anger reflected in Glenlillian's eyes, and knew Kim was in trouble yet again.

The journey into the dark forest was made in utter silence. King Crawford's knights and soldiers followed the fey guards without complaint and, after many hours searching the densest areas, they came upon the small encampment of King William's servants.

"Here, Mr. Smithers. Sit down, and I will tend to your wounded foot."

"Thank God in heaven you found us, Sir James. We were all about to lose hope of ever being found."

"Nonsense. You think King William does not have friends? Friends who knew you were all missing? King Crawford came quickly to take back Castle Mead for King William, and sent us in all haste to fetch all of you."

"He is a good King, Sir James. But could you tell me, please, what are those strange, small creatures over there by Sir Richard?"

"No, Mr. Smithers. Your eyes do not deceive you. They are male fairies. But whatever you do, do not call them fairies. They are called fey and they are all very skilled knights." Mr. Smithers could only nod his head, so stunned was he at the sight before him.

The king's people were being fed. And the fey guards tended to the wounds some received from spider bites, sunburn, scrapes and scratches from branches, and twisted ankles from falls. The knights were setting up tents to cover them from the storm brewing in the distance, and ordered the women and children into them.

The fey guards brought many hooded cloaks and covered the men servants. The cloaks were made of a particular material that allowed them to expand to meet the size of the wearer. They offered protection from the elements. The knights, soldiers and men servants were stunned by such a garment, and could only nod a thank you.

Jahaziel was satisfied that all was being done as the king requested, so he went in search of Kim. He assured Glenlillian he would not stop looking until he had found her daughter.

Finally, he broke through the western edge of the dark forest, and continued on with the light of a full moon guiding him. He headed in the direction back to Crawford's castle using the smaller main road as a shortcut, used by travelers going and coming on trade routes.

He heard the sound of an eagle high above him, and strained his neck to look up to see it. Jahaziel realized the bird was following him, and he stopped his horse just in time to watch the decent. Jahaziel quickly lifted his arms over his head in a gesture of protection as the bird swooped down toward him. This caused his horse to prance in agitation.

To his disbelief, the large bird landed on his arm, fluttered its wings once, and then settled down with one last screech. He slowly lowered his arm, and was eye-to-eye with the large bird. That was when he saw the ring hooked onto the eagle's beak. Jahaziel held out his right-hand and turned his palm upward, and then the eagle dropped the ring into it.

"Show me where she is," Jahaziel said softly. The eagle took flight. At Jahaziel's urging, his horse leapt into a run, and followed the soaring eagle.

King Crawford paced back and forth in front of the drawbridge. He was so oblivious to the downpour, thunder and lightning, he did not hear King William's approach. He jumped at the sound of his name, and looked at the king, stunned.

William grabbed him in a breath-expelling bear hug and slapped him on his back saying, "I am sorry it has taken me so long to get here, Crawford. Walk with me. I have to tell you a story very much in need of an explanation."

They walked slowly toward the entrance to Castle Mead, deep in conversation, with the weight of shared responsibility upon them. This young, newly appointed king, and the older, seasoned king, would solve the problems of their kingdoms together with a newly formed friendship.

"You say Joyce was well when Sir Gauwain left her?" Crawford asked, as he warmed his hands by the fire of the entrance hall. His worry diminished as he waited for William to answer.

"Yes. It was his intent all along to keep her safe. I need a promise from you Crawford that you will not harm this knight. He should not be punished for protecting your wife."

"Does Gauwain think I am so inept that I cannot protect my own wife?" he roared.

"No, no. Of course not. What he does know, is what Arnault is about, and he could not take the chance he was being followed by Arnault's henchmen. Gauwain suspected Arnault did not completely trust him, and with good reason. He knew Gauwain had served me and had agreed to the exchange for my nephew. I believe he was testing Gauwain's loyalty, since I was the one who banished him the first time.

"After the battle at Newry, his servants were sent to serve me, and his home was burned to the ground as a punishment. He had planned to take over that land and claim it for his own with the intent to rebuild what he had lost. Newry belongs to no man, and it will stay that way. I will ensure it remains uninhabited and untouched—protected and preserved for its beauty as long as I continue to be caretaker.

"Go fetch your wife, Crawford. I will stay here and straighten out what is left of this mess," King William advised.

"The rest of my men have been sent for, and should be

arriving tomorrow, and some days after. Arnault will rue the day he decided to tangle with me, and take what is mine. He will be stripped of his title and all he holds dear. What of this golden chalice, Crawford? Has Arnault gotten his hands on it?" King William asked.

"I do not think he has had any luck in that matter."

King Crawford bowed to King William, and then left in all haste to go to his wife. He promised William he would not kill Sir Gauwain, allowing the knight to accompany him on the journey to fetch his wife.

Now, with fresh horses, they left in a thunderous cloud of pounding hooves, amidst the shouting, thunder, lightning, and the deluge of rain that pelted them.

Chapter Eight

Kim, Mr. and Mrs. Jones, and the queen, smiled down at the beautiful little baby girl. Her fine strands of reddish-blonde hair stuck out all over, giving her a very comical appearance. Her eye color could not be determined since she refused to open them. The biggest surprise in her appearance, however, was the color of her skin—a pale light pink that was in contrast to the queen's darker skin.

They all had tears in their eyes, and they made up silly, nonsensical words to coax the baby into smiling. The baby was warmly wrapped in a beautiful little blanket given to her by Mrs. Jones. Queen Joyce held her treasure tightly to her, leaned her head back, and fell asleep in what Sir Gauwain called his lounging chair.

"She is clearly exhausted, Miss Fairy. Should we leave her be now?" Mrs. Jones whispered in a thick accent Kim was not familiar with.

She smiled at the servant. "My name is Kim, and you may address me so."

"Should I bring her something to eat, Miss Kim?"

"Do you have some clear broth with a few vegetables in it perhaps?" Kim asked. "She should not eat a heavy meal after just giving birth. But it did not seem overly difficult for her to accomplish. Do you not think, Mrs. Jones?"

"Yes, I have freshly made broth downstairs in the kitchen. And, no, she did not have a difficult time of it, thanks to you. You say she is a queen?"

Kim nodded yes, and Mrs. Jones went down to the kitchen to fetch the broth. Her husband tended to the fire again, to make sure the queen and her new little princess were warm and comfortable. Then he went downstairs to help his wife. Kim stayed behind, and cleaned up the room while she pondered what she had just witnessed. *How strong this woman was to do what she had done.*

Kim recalled how, like the deer in the field, Queen Joyce had labored. With quiet words, during her labor she had told Kim, "I do not wish to distress this baby by shouting, but by all the heavens I truly wish to."

When she was satisfied with the results of her cleaning, Kim sat close to the sleeping queen and baby. She leaned over, and touched the princess' soft face.

Shortly after, Mrs. Jones quietly opened the chamber room door, but stopped momentarily. She wiped away tears of happiness with her apron, and looked upon the queen, the princess, and the fairy sleeping away their exhaustion on Sir Gauwain's lounging chair.

She covered the bowl of broth she had brought with her, and set it on the small table next to the chair. She looked around and found a cover, which she placed gently over them. Then she joined her husband below chambers to eat the supper she had prepared.

The baby started fussing, which awoke Kim from her slumber. Kim smiled at the sounds the baby made. The baby tried to look at her.

"She cannot see as of yet, Kim. But she can see the light around you, and she will try to focus," the new mother said.

Kim sat up, and touched her wings to turn off the light. She conversed quietly with Queen Joyce for more than an hour. She told her everything she knew and could remember. When she had finished, she heard the queen defending Sir Gauwain.

"I believe what you say, Queen Joyce," Kim responded. "I was told earlier by his servants that Sir Gauwain did not set the fire, and that he saved King William's people by suggesting they be sent into the dark forest. Sir Gauwain is very close to Mr. and Mrs. Jones, and I am told he discusses many matters with them. As horrible a place as that forest is, I do not think they would have been followed. I hope, nay, pray, your husband does not harm Sir Gauwain before he can explain himself."

Kim and the queen continued speaking to one another a while longer. And from that moment on, they were the best of friends. Even though Kim was a fairy, she was also female, and Joyce could speak to her about her concerns and things women enjoy discussing—love, children, clothes, and secrets.

The queen asked Kim if she was rested enough to go to her husband and tell him where she was, but to please not mention the baby. It was to be her surprise.

Queen Joyce leaned her head back to rest again, and smiled at the thought of her husband seeing the baby for the first time. It was her last thought before going into a much-needed, deep sleep. In her dreams, she saw her baby as older—laughing and playing outside the castle grounds. And the look of pure happiness upon her face showed her joy.

Kim turned on her wing lights once again, and headed out of Sir Gauwain's keep. At the sound of horse and eagle, she stopped and spotted Jahaziel as he burst out of the thick woods. Kim looked up, waved a thank you to her new-found raptor friend, and slowly directed her gaze to Jahaziel, who was quickly approaching.

When he reached her, and the dust cleared, he could be heard yelling with such furious words that birds left the safe haven of the trees in immediate response.

"What are you doing up there? Come down here this minute!" he demanded.

Kim shook her head no, and flew up even farther away.

Jahaziel realized his angry words had startled Kim. He closed his eyes, and said in a softer voice, "You women will be the death of me. Come down here, Kim. I am not angry."

She hesitated for a few moments, and then did as Jahaziel asked. He grabbed her so fast she could not stop him. He turned her around and around, all the while asking, "Are you OK? Are you hurt? Are you ill? Are you insane? Do not dare cry, for I will throttle you if you do."

His last words were no more than a whisper. He did not realize he was hugging her until she spoke with laughter in her voice. "You are crushing me, Jahaziel. Let me go."

He quickly released her and waited for her explanation. When she did not speak, he did.

"I nearly killed myself getting here. What is so important that you sent my ring to me?" He shoved his ring back into her hand, and waited for her explanation.

"Come down off your horse and follow me," she said. Her smile never left her face while he climbed the stairs. She put the ring back onto her wrist, and then floated next to him.

Jahaziel was so stunned at the sight before him that he fell to his knees in homage to his queen and newborn princess.

Kim began to speak in a whispered voice so as not to awaken the sleeping mother and child. "I was hoping you would arrive before the birthing, for I was truly frightened for her and the baby," she said.

Jahaziel looked at Kim, stunned, and spoke with a strained voice. "You sent for me to help with the birthing? Have you completely lost your mind? Or, did you have an accident which could explain your idiotic notion?"

Kim could not understand Jahaziel's anger and quietly strained words.

"You do not know how to assist in the birthing of human babies?"

He shook his head back and forth, a clear no his only answer, for he was truly speechless.

Kim patted his arm, and said, "Do not be embarrassed. I did not know much of the subject myself, and was not prepared for the sudden delivery. Had I not had enough time to mix the potion used for the relaxing of muscles, I think Queen Joyce would have had a much more difficult delivery. And to think, had my small hands not fit so perfectly around that little bundle to gently turn her around, she would have come out feet first. And the queen…"

Kim's words were smothered by Jahaziel's fingers covering her entire face.

"Please, tell me no more of this. I cannot take this talk of birthing," he said to Kim.

With her eyes wide, and her nod of yes, she moved away from him. Jahaziel stood, then quickly walked down the steps and out the castle doors.

The sound of thunder in the distance had Jahaziel looking toward the forest. He knew well what a large contingency of men on horses sounded like.

He mounted his stallion, and rode to meet his king. He was truly glad for the reprieve from women's—and the fairy's—complaints. He welcomed the friendship of other men, and talk of other things.

His mind momentarily brought the face of the baby princess forward, and he could not help smiling. That was how King Crawford found his best knight—smiling.

This caused the king to frown, and he roared his words. “Jahaziel, explain yourself!”

Chapter Nine

As dawn approached, the last of the king's soldiers filed out of Sir Gauwain's upper chamber—Jahaziel being the last to leave. The king and queen were left alone to be together to celebrate the birth of their baby. They had named her Teri.

Just as Jahaziel silently closed the door behind him, he overheard the queen speak of her troubles with Agnes, and her worries that she might be appointed nanny.

Jahaziel always enjoyed watching the sunrise—with its golden light's shining approach that promised a new day and a fresh start. He lifted his head, closed his eyes, and enjoyed the feel of warmth and light.

"Forgive me for the interruption, Jahaziel, but it is time that I return home," a quiet voice said.

Jahaziel opened his eyes, and spoke in a soft whisper. "Kim, it was your mother who sent me to look for you, and I think you should not go home alone. She seemed upset, and told me how angry your father was that you had left without telling anyone where you would be going. Would you like me to go with you?"

"No. Thank you for the offer, but I have some flower and herb gathering to do first. My mother loves flowers, and is always seeking out new herbs for healing. Perhaps a peace offering would help calm my mother's anger. I do not suppose you have a little trinket on you that I could give my father?" Kim asked.

Jahaziel's hearty laughter gave Kim her answer.

"I do not know how I manage to get into so much trouble,"

she said. “But I seem to vex my parents more often these days. Oh, before I forget, I am to tell you that you are not to harm Sir Gauwain. The queen wishes this, as do I.”

Jahaziel watched Kim’s departure until she disappeared through the woods and was out of his sight.

Jahaziel was able to speak with Sir Gauwain alone. He was content with the complete telling of the siege at Castle Mead. Kim’s last words to him rang in his ears, and he had given her his promise he would not harm the knight.

“Gauwain, I should knock you senseless just on principle. If one more person or fairy tells me not to kill you, I promise it will be their last words,” Sir Jahaziel remarked.

Gauwain’s booming laughter made Jahaziel laugh in response. As he settled his mind once again to all that had taken place, he was content knowing the end justified the means.

King Crawford’s men understood Sir Gauwain had a hand in saving the life of the Queen and her child, and they thanked him for his bravery and quick thinking. This act, however started, saved Sir Gauwain, his home, and his title, and ended his contract with King Arnault.

Both knights were grateful for the sight of Mr. Jones approaching them holding two large containers of mead. Filled to their brims, the mead splashed over the edges with each hurried step Mr. Jones took.

“You surely are a sight for sore eyes, Mr. Jones.” Gauwain took the container offered him and drank deeply. Jahaziel thanked Mr. Jones, and did the same.

The knights stopped their conversation when a squealing sound drew their attention. They were very surprised to see a plump, little guinea pig sitting on the ground so close to them.

Lulu Piggy had traveled the long distance to the old castle

ruin on the back of a tamed wolf for the soul purpose of speaking to Jahaziel. She had overheard Kim's parents arguing about Kim sneaking away without telling anyone where she was going.

Lulu had understood their intent to send Kim away to a neighboring clan, to "learn a few lessons of responsibility." So she decided to warn Kim by seeking the knight's help.

Her little eyes glinted at the memory of the heated words, and her mind went back to the conversation between Kim's parents.

"What do you mean you cannot find her?" Luther had yelled at his wife.

"If you think yelling at me is going to get you an answer, think again," his wife had retorted.

"I am sorry, Glen, but I have had just about enough of her irresponsibility. She has no care for her safety. She cannot go running off whenever the notion hits her. She has been accepted by Huw, and needs to learn a few lessons of responsibility before their ceremony.

I have decided to send her to your sister's clan. Since Gwendolyn has no children, perhaps she will be immune to Kim's charms and discipline her properly."

Glenlillian had been too angry with Luther to agree or disagree with him, and had flown away to find solace in her favorite garden.

Lulu's thoughts came back to the present. She knew that the knight would not understand her, but her hope was that he would know something was wrong.

Jahaziel bent down to the ground and patted Lulu on the head, while speaking softly so as not to frighten the creature. "I must assume Kim has sent you to me, or you wish to tell me something is amiss?"

Lulu jumped up and down, and squealed loudly at his words of "something amiss."

"Is Kim in trouble again?" Jahaziel whispered. Lulu squealed all the louder, content that the knight assumed correctly.

Jahaziel scooped up the guinea pig, once again entered Gauwain's castle, mounted the stairs, and spoke quietly with the king and queen. He voiced his concerns that Kim's parents were angry that she had ventured so far without thought of danger or concern of what she would find when she came here.

"You must go and speak with her parents, and thank Kim properly, Crawford." Queen Joyce spoke to her husband. And he could not help seeing her tear-filled eyes.

"Her concern for us overshadowed her common sense. If she had any fear or reservations about being here, it was not evident to me. She did not speak of her own troubles, and took charge like a well-trained knight. I found her company to be very welcoming. Please go with Jahaziel. Teri and I will be fine. Besides, I cannot travel as of yet, and Mr. and Mrs. Jones have been taking good care of us. If it makes you feel better, leave Sir Gauwain here with some of your men."

King Crawford finally relented, letting his wife have her way. He kissed her, kissed his new baby girl, barked orders to all around him, and rode away from the small castle, heading in the direction Jahaziel knew Kim had gone.

Mrs. Jones had just enough time to get out of the king's way before she entered Gauwain's chamber, proud she had not spilled one ounce of the soup or the water she carried. Smiling, she spoke, "Your Majesty, was that a knight carrying a guinea cava?" Their shared laughter echoed down the stairs and out into the hallway.

Not knowing where the guinea pig lived, Jahaziel decided to bring her with him to Luther and Glenlillian's home. With great care, he placed Lulu securely into a pouch that hung from his saddle. The pouch was filled with soft cloths and a carrot. He smiled at the clicking sound she made as she snuggled down. Moments later, Lulu was fast asleep.

As the sun climbed higher in the sky, its sparkling light danced through the thickness of the forest trees allowing a better view for the king and knight as they traveled in silence. Keeping their thoughts to themselves, each contemplated what they would say to the parents of this unique fairy called Kim.

Then the sound of shouting broke their reverie.

"You come back here this minute young lady. I am not finished speaking to you!"

"Luther, you are not speaking to your daughter, you are shouting at her. Do you honestly think she would stand here and listen to you?" Glenlillian responded.

"She needs to understand her whereabouts are to be known at all times. She cannot gallivant about thoughtlessly. She is my daughter—the daughter of the fey king of Phenloris—and she does not behave as a royal fairy should."

"Hush, husband. You are working yourself into an anger you will be sorry for later. Kim is too old to change her ways now. You must settle your mind to the fact Kim is Kim, and I would not have her be any different."

"Yes, you would say this to me now. But she has angered you as well and the tables are turned. Are they not? You were yelling a fairy trouble upon Kim just moments before," the king argued.

So deep were they into this shouting match, neither saw the knight and king on horseback at their front door until the sound of a horse's snort startled them. More shouting came from Luther, demanding they explain their sudden appearance.

Kim listened to all this, all the while crying softly to herself. Her decision to seek out Egwin for advice was not to be made in haste. She worried what her father might do if he found her missing once again.

She could not believe her mother could be heard yelling for all to hear that Kim should have nine daughters just like her. What was wrong with her that she would be so upsetting to her own mother that she would say such a thing? And where exactly did the number nine come from? Fairies had one child at a time, and rarely had more than two.

Kim began to cry much harder when a thought occurred to her that Huw might have heard her mother and might want to break their announcement. This upset Kim even more, and she sat down on a pile of soft heather and cried until she started hiccupping.

The sound of Jahaziel's voice echoing throughout the garden snapped Kim out of her sorrowful thoughts. It was clear to her that Jahaziel was angry with her father. They yelled back and forth without either stopping to take a breath between their shouting.

"Do not tell me how to handle my daughter, sir knight. This is none of your business," Luther argued.

"You dare speak to me this way after all that has happened?" Jahaziel asked. "You do not deserve this woman you call daughter."

She quickly wiped at her face, and rushed back to her home. Kim broke through the forest and into their small garden, and then came to a sudden stop, quite startled to be face-to-face with King Crawford.

King Crawford ignored her father and Jahaziel, and smiled at Kim with all the warmth and kindness he had in his heart. He did not miss the tears in Kim's eyes.

He also noticed how much taller she was than her mother, how she did not resemble either parent, and how her red face did not mar her beauty.

The yelling immediately stopped as King Crawford dismounted his stallion.

Just inches away from the hovering fairy, he slowly knelt on the ground, placed his right hand over his heart, his left hand on the hilt of his sword, and spoke in a firm and commanding voice for all to hear. "I, Crawford William Martin George Fitzhuwlyn, king of the realm, north, south, east, and west, of the great forest, and land holder of King Edward's Allenwood Castle and domain, and protector of the land of Newry, do hereby kneel before this fairy known as Kimberlyn, and pledge my loyalty, honor, and promises made as binding and law.

"I say also, with her permission, that Joyce Doreen Murphy Allen Fitzhuwlyn, my wife and queen of this same realm, pledges her loyalty, honor, and promises made to be also binding to the fairy known as Kim.

"I hereto, also extend to her family, descendants, and creatures within the Phenloris clan the same pledge and promises. I say and do this without coercion, and of my own free will in thanksgiving for her bravery and assistance with the birth of my daughter, and her kindness toward my wife, Queen Joyce."

After dismounting his horse, Jahaziel knelt next to his king and repeated his pledge of loyalty, honor, and promises made to also be binding and of his own free will, without coercion, to the fairy known as Kim. He did not, however, extended his pledge to Luther.

None were aware of Huw's presence until he went to his betrothed. With his arms around her, Kim cried all the more, holding onto Huw as if her life depended on him and him alone. Her parents were speechless, and could only stare at the now-standing king and knight.

Jahaziel gently handed the guinea pig to Glenlillian, stared at Huw a moment, and mounted his horse. Both men quietly left the area.

Chapter Ten

Glenlillian combed her daughter's long, straight hair and adjusted the golden cloak around her shoulders.

Hardly able to speak, she handed Kim a box, and said in a shaky voice, "This is a gift from King Crawford and Queen Joyce. The queen said to tell you that, although they were not permitted to witness your ceremony, they wanted you to have something memorable to remember this day for many years. It is their special thank you for your help and friendship."

Kim looked at her mother, and slowly opened the beautifully crafted box. On the inside of the lid were hand-carved creatures of the forest—a rabbit, guinea pig, fox, hawk, and a small plant that looked like Patience.

Kim smiled at the memory of Patience insisting on living with Queen Joyce. Kim gave in to her request, and said her goodbyes to her favorite walking plant.

Glenlillian saw her daughter's tears, and both stared in silent wonder at the breathtakingly beautiful tiny, gold, jewel-encrusted tiara resting upon a blue, silk pillow. Nestled next to the tiara was a rolled parchment with King Crawford's seal. With gentle care, Kim broke the seal, unrolled the parchment, and then read the hand-written poem.

We send our love with grateful praise,
this day you have been chosen.
A golden gift to all your clan,
upon their lips your name forever spoken.

You are now known as Kimberlyn, Gold Fairy,
a title bestowed with great caring.
A deserving appointment for one so young,
that you embrace with regal bearing.
All our love to you, signed,
Crawford, Joyce and Baby Teri.

Kim burst into tears, and Glenlillian hugged her daughter for a long moment. Finally, she wiped her face saying, "You do not want your ceremony remembered as you having watery eyes and a red nose do you? Stop crying now, and let me put this beautiful coronet on your head."

Kim did as her mother said, and looked at her reflection in the ancient mirror. The jewels upon her head sparkled in colorful brilliance, and the bracelet ring on her wrist shone with splendid beauty, giving Kim an ethereal appearance.

The golden cloak and dress, handmade by an unknown elf—though Kim had her suspicions it was her elf—finished the splendid attire. Her mother's own crystal tiara shone with a magical array of brilliant light that took Kim's breath away. And she was pleased to see her mother dressed in her own ceremonial garments.

Kim nodded her head and, taking her mother's hand in hers, they glided out together toward the meadow where the entire fairy clan of Phenloris assembled to celebrate this special day.

Kim stopped at the foot of a platform, curtsied to her father, and rose up to hover before him. Luther was elegantly dressed as well, and upon his head was the great crown of the fey king of Phenloris. His pride in his daughter showed on his face, and with a quick wink of love, he lifted the golden chalice high in the air and spoke in the ancient language of fairies.

This elixir, contained within the sacred chalice, held the properties of a multitude of magic and was not to be taken lightly. When he finished his litany, he handed the chalice to Kim. She drank deeply, then handed it back to her father. The mist encircled Kim, and new powers began to form within her as their strength increased. The loud voices of her clan were heard cheering in unison.

"Kimberlyn, gold fairy! Kimberlyn, gold fairy! Kimberlyn, gold fairy!"

Glenlillian's tears of happiness and pride were quickly replaced with tears of sadness. For her only daughter was now grown, and crowned gold fairy.

It was at this precise moment that she remembered her rushed, harsh words spoken in anger when she discovered Kim had once again gone off on her own without telling anyone where she had been heading. Her mind recalled that moment, and how she had focused in on her anger, and the words that had spewed forth were not planned.

"You have driven me to such distraction, that I have mixed up the recipes of two important poison ivy and oak pastes," her mother had said. "They are completely different from one another and, if confused in the preparation, they cure neither condition.

"Your father wants to send you to your aunt Gwendolyn for a very long stay. Personally, I am inclined to agree with him, Kim. Perhaps you should have nine daughters just like you to torment you to the end of your days, Kimberlyn. Then, and only then, will you understand how upsetting you can be at times. You must always tell us where you are going."

The words could not be taken back or removed, for when a crystal fairy strongly stated anything close to a command it was done instantly. But instead of holding her head in shame, Glenlillian had burst out in joyous laughter at the thought of Kim with nine daughters just like her. And she had laughed all the more when she had recalled Kim's reaction.

"Mother. What have you done? You cannot take those

words back."

The only response from Glenlillian had been an outburst of laughter, and a hearty, "Oops."

Clapping her hands together, Glenlillian lifted her dress and flew toward the sound of fey menfolk singing, drinking, and boasting of feats not true. She was in search of her husband.

She found him at the edge of the meadow in deep conversation with Huw. She had made up her mind to persuade Luther to take her with him on his next adventure—after the nine fairy grandbabies were born, of course.

"Broadwayne, come with me," Luther commanded.

The fey guard followed Luther to the abandoned fairy hut where the fey traitor had remained guarded. Unable to join in the festivities, his mind had boiled into an uncontrollable anger.

"I see being locked up has not cooled your temper in the least bit, Maximilian," Luther said. "I demand to know why you spoke of our golden chalice to a human. You know our laws better than any here. You have been given a double title—fey guard and keeper of laws. Are these titles not enough of an honor that you would seek out a human to boast of your knowledge?"

"You think I would speak to disgusting humans? I spoke to no human," Maximilian said. "I spoke to an elf in need of information. He was desperate to save his wife and a friend ill with an undetermined disease. He paid me well for this information, and I told him where to find the golden chalice."

"You idiot!" Luther roared. "He told a human called Arnault."

Luther turned to Broadwayne, and said, "Go fetch my wife."

Maximilian's eyes grew wide, and he tried to escape. Rushing forward with arms and hands extended, he tried to hurl

Broadwayne and Luther out the door.

In the blink of an eye, fey restraint webbing flung at Max, and he hung in the air completely wrapped in the webbing. He swung gently back and forth as a single strand held him dangling from the pine bark rafters.

Glenlillian was laughing so hard from the loud, ridiculously bold lies being told to her of adventures not true, that she nearly fell off the rock wall where she sat. She enjoyed the feys' abilities to think up such lavish lies on the spot.

Her laughter vanished when Broadwayne whispered in her ear to follow him.

"I cannot do this, Luther." she said as she flitted back and forth in front of him. "You must understand this is a permanent, irreversible action. What if Maximilian has a change of heart at the last minute? I cannot undue an encasement once it is done."

"You think I do not know this? You think I make this decision frivolously?" Luther replied.

"Calm yourself, husband. I did not mean to insult you. I think we should have more discussion on the matter."

"Glen. Maximilian is trussed up like a batch of herbs. He cannot stay there while we talk."

"I do not know what else we can do to contain him. Let me think, Luther."

"I can help you, father." Kim's words were a surprise and a shock, and both parents answered in unison.

"What do you mean you can help? Explain."

"I can send him to a place of darkness where he cannot escape. It is a dark containment where he will be free to be, and think. He will need no food or drink, as this place is a pause in living. It is called Nothingness," she explained.

Clearly shocked by her words, the questions flew from her parents, tumbling like pebbles in a moving river. Kim could not understand them. She raised her hand, and bellowed, "Stop all this yelling. Do you wish me to do this or not?"

Luther spoke before Glenlillian could. "Do this now, Kim. But you will explain all when you are finished."

"Yes, of course. You must go outside. Please, do not speak. I must concentrate."

As they stood outside, Kim remained in the doorway. The look on Maximilian's face showed his fear.

"You will not feel pain, Max. Close your eyes," she ordered him.

He did as she ordered.

Kim looked to the cloudless sky, closed her eyes, and spoke in the ancient fairy language. Her words were not understood by her parents, nor by Broadwayne.

Kim reached behind her back and pulled out a fireball the size of a large cooking pot. She threw it forward, directly at Maximilian. Then she had just enough time to turn around and yell, "Fly! Quickly!"

The explosion, heard for many miles around, had feys and fairies flying toward the sound at high speed. The large crowd hovered behind Kim, Broadwayne and her parents in silence. The only words from Kim's mouth were a near-whisper. "I think the hut went with him."

"There is nothing here to see. Everyone go back to the celebrations. Musicians, play, play," Broadwayne ordered. He then followed the startled clan gatherers as they slowly floated back to the celebration.

As whisperings broke out among them, they asked each other questions that could not be answered.

Kim began to shake, and her father sat her gently on a boulder, holding her until she was calm again.

"Sweetling. I am in great need of an explanation. I do not understand this Nothingness you speak of, nor your ability to conjure forth such a large ball of fire. How has this happened? Explain how this knowledge has come to you?" Her father was full of questions.

Kim took a deep breath, looked tiredly at her father, and said, "The golden chalice."

Kim managed to persuade her father to let her be alone for a few minutes.

As he stood, he turned to her, and said, "You are an amazing creature and I still cannot believe you are my daughter." His eyes glistened with unshed tears, and a smile remained on his face as he quietly glided away to join Glenlillian and the others.

When Kim was assured she was alone, she went to the place she had sent Maximilian.

Touching her wing lights, Kim entered the hut, and was relieved to see Max still hanging in the fey webbing, gently swaying back and forth. She raised her hands and clicked her fingers, and Max fell to the floor. He immediately jumped up and, with great speed, flew at Kim.

Kim did not move, and Max slammed into an invisible shield. He then flew backwards, hit the far wall of the hut, and slipped into unconsciousness.

Satisfied that he was no longer bound by the webbing, Kim turned around and headed out of Nothingness, taking every bit of light with her.

Six moons had passed since Princess Teri was born, and Kim was free to visit as often as her duties as gold fairy would allow her.

Kim, I am so very excited for you," the Queen had told her. "I hope you and Huw will be very happy together. When people decide to be together for the rest of their lives they become engaged first, and then marry. But, I think I like your word better. Acceptance seems so romantically sweeter. When will this celebration take place?"

"When the spring solstice announces itself, and comes with the blooming of the cherries," Kim answered her. "Beautiful white flowers fall from trees that were planted in ancient days, and cover the ground with a continuous flow. There is a meadow used for clan meetings that has hundreds of cherry trees surrounding it. We will have our acceptance ceremony there. And, if my father times it correctly, we should be showered with the blooms just as he finishes reading from the Book of Acceptance."

"I do not suppose the king and I are allowed to come witness your acceptance," the queen inquired.

"I am sad to say 'no' to you and the king, for my father has forbidden humans to witness our ceremonies. He said terrible things would happen if they did—something he calls rightful vanishing. I do not know of this, but he is my father and king of our clan. I cannot go against his demand. Well, I mostly cannot."

The fairy and the queen burst out laughing, with the secret knowledge that Kim did not always do what her father demanded.

"Joyce, is something wrong?" Kim asked her. "I see your pensive look just now. Perhaps I can help."

"It is all this business with Agnes. Just when I thought things were going well with her, I hear more complaints from servants and others. I had to make a difficult decision."

Kim's questioning look told the queen that she could trust her.

"This all started not long after the birth of Teri," the queen said, recalling for Kim her conversation with Agnes nearly word for word.

"Agnes, do you understand what I am saying to you? The King and I agree you need time away from all of us. I think the influences of court have had a negative effect on you, and you are not yourself. I have received many complaints of late from servants, knights and traders about your behavior," Queen Joyce had said.

"What complaints?" Agnes had quipped.

"That is no longer important. What is important is your negative attitude. Crawford and I think you are not happy here with us. Your complaints are many."

"I am happy enough, but there is much to complain about. Your new cook cannot cook. Your maids spend all their time gossiping instead of cleaning and preparing rooms for guests. The knights..."

"Enough!" Queen Joyce had commanded.

"I did not want to go into this, but these are some of the complaints leveled against you," the queen had told Agnes. "When you are asked to help, you do not, and think cleaning is beneath you. You gossip with whoever is in earshot, and tell the most outrageous lies. You cannot be trusted with a confidence, and you have become overbearing."

Queen Joyce had taken a deep breath, and had continued, "Mrs. Smith and Miss Taylor spotted an empty cottage three miles from here. It has been scrubbed from top to bottom, and has been filled with plenty of necessities, including your personal things. I have put my own mark on the cottage with decorations from my own personal collection of furniture, pictures, kitchen essentials, tapestries, and books," the queen had told her.

"Everything is ready for you, and regular supplies will be

sent. If anything else is needed you may give a note to the supply carrier. You will live there until you can come to your senses and change your attitude and bad behavior." Joyce had closed her eyes, and waited for the shouting she knew would come.

But it hadn't.

Agnes had then spoken in a low, spite-filled voice. Each word had been said with a slow anger, as her eyes had become mere slits in her head.

"I have been to that cottage."

"Really? Then you know it is not an unpleasant place in which to make a home for yourself."

"I have visited the cottage many times thinking to retire there one day. I will not oppose you or the king to send me now. But mark my words, I will have my day. When it comes, you will all be very sorry."

"You dare threaten me, Agnes?"

"No. You misunderstand me. It is your own haughty behavior that will come back to threaten you. You will sorrow on that day."

Queen Joyce had finished her words, and had waited for Kim to answer.

"Joyce. I believe you have made the right decision. Do not berate yourself and worry so," Kim had said to comfort her.

"I suppose you are right, besides there is much celebration coming your way, and I know you need to go. Thank you for stopping by to see me. May I give you a gift before you go, Kim?"

"Joyce, it is not necessary."

"It is tradition to give a bride a gift. It brings the couple good luck."

Queen Joyce rose, and walked to a far wall in her receiving

room where her handmade chest was located. She opened it, and removed a jeweled belt and a piece of sheer, white material that had sparkled from the colorful variety of gems hand-sewn into it.

She had handed it to Kim, and spoke with a shaking voice. "This belt is for Huw, and the veil is for you to put over your hair with the coronet on top. I had it made to match. When you wear these, I hope you will think of us warmly, and know we are your friends, and will be for our lifetimes."

Kim had burst into tears, and the queen had joined in.

As the queen walked out of the castle with Kim floating next to her, they had said their goodbyes.

"Wait, Kim." The queen ran back to her and, as she tried to catch her breath, she stammered, "Jahaziel gave me this letter to give to you. He said to read it after the ceremony."

Stunned, Kim took the letter, and headed home to prepare for her acceptance ceremony, festivities, and fairy games.

Chapter Eleven

Several moons had passed since Kimberlyn's crowning ceremony, and this morning was charged with much excitement as the fairy clan of Phenloris began the preparations for the acceptance gathering.

The clan was also host for the spring solstice celebrations.

Every clan, from sea to sea, assembled, mingled, ate, drank and helped prepare decorations for the festivities. Miles of tables were covered with food of every sort, and many vessels filled with Glenlillian's special brew were lined up, one after the other, for all to enjoy.

Kim looked at herself in the ancient mirror of her dressing room, and was pleased she chose to wear the dress of her golden crowning celebration. Glenlillian had curled her hair the night before, and Kim loved the results. She placed her jewel-encrusted coronet, with its matching veil, onto her head.

With a deep sigh, she wondered at how much time had passed since meeting Jahaziel, who had been injured and near death, in the woods near Crawford's keep and castle. Why, it seemed like only yesterday that they had become such great friends. She wondered why many of the fairy clans had avoided contact with people, and continued to do so. She found their company delightful, and the stories they told her were outrageously funny.

It was, however, her father's command that the fairy clan of Phenloris limit their exposure to those humans who were already aware of their existence, and not show themselves at all to people they did not know.

Luther stood tall and, looking very handsome, according to Kim and her mother, began his reading. “We, the fairy clan of Phenloris, are gathered here with many fairy clans to celebrate the announcement of my daughter Kimberlyn, gold fairy princess, to Huw, first fey guard and harp maker.”

He then whispered to Kim and Huw, saying, “Please face each other and repeat these words.”

Fey and fairy smiled at each other, and spoke with love and great sincerity in their voices. “We will always find magic separately, yet find it to be stronger as we are one. The magic of family, love, and children. Magic of friends, of stars, and the sun. We are stronger when together, and weaker when apart, and on this day of our announcement we are now one, as if one heart.”

Huw placed the gold promised ring, with its ornate design of two knots intertwining, on the middle finger of Kim’s left hand. And Kim returned the gesture by placing the matching ring onto Huw’s middle finger of his left hand.

Their kiss lasted long moments and, as the blooms from the cherry trees fell like the snow of winter, the loud cheers of the assembled clan echoed into the darkest of forests. The newly joined couple walked to their family and friends, accepting congratulations and gifts.

Then came the time for the planting of the Concordia promised seed. The entire clan followed Kim and Huw into the garden, singing the fairy birthing songs along with a few bawdy fey guard songs, as laughter broke out among the gathered assembly.

Shyly, Kim and Huw walked deeper into the garden to pick a spot to plant their seed.

"Did you remember to bring the fey dust, Huw?"

"How could I not? And how about you, did you bring your fairy dust?"

They burst out laughing, and finally came upon an isolated area free from other Concordia's. Satisfied this was the perfect spot, Kim and Huw knelt down.

They removed the soil and, as they sprinkled their dust upon the open ground, spoke in unison. "Here is the planting and our wish of new dreams. A promise made, with the exchanging of rings. May peace be forever upon the seed we lay here, and fey/fairy spring forth without any fear."

With their hands joined, they covered the Concordia promised seed, patted the soil, and stood, as more congratulations came from their clan.

Then, as the wonderful day began to drift into evening, Kim and Huw found a quiet place to be alone and talk.

"You look so handsome in your new coat, Huw. Do you like your belt?"

"Kim, I find it to be a singularly beautiful thing to behold. And your veil is stunning. The first chance we get, we must go and thank them properly."

"Really? You would go with me?"

"We are together now, why would I not go with you?"

"I am so used to doing things on my own. I sometimes worry my parents. You might not know this, and it may be too late now, but I get into trouble a lot, and…Are you laughing at me?"

Huw's laughter broke the quietness, and the birds nesting in the nearby trees left in angry swiftness in search of farther quiet havens.

"I am sorry sweet, but your father gave me a lecture on your shortcomings. And, I had to stop him. He seemed to enjoy giving me a litany of your faults," Huw answered.

With her hands on her hips, Kim rose quickly, then stopped just as suddenly, causing Jahaziel's letter to fall out of a pocket and onto the ground.

Huw bent down, retrieved the letter and tried to open it. Kim was swift, and yanked it out of his hands. Her face was red, and she was clearly embarrassed.

"What is going on here, Kim?" Huw asked.

"This is a letter from Sir Jahaziel, and I have yet to read it," she stammered.

"Why are you so rattled about this letter? Do you know what he writes?"

"No." Her blush grew, and Huw put his hand out.

"Before I read this letter, is there something you want to tell me?" he asked her.

Kim took a breath, and closed her eyes. She would not look at Huw while she spoke. "You know the story of Jahaziel, and how my mother and I tended to his injuries?"

Lifting one eyebrow, his words told her to go on. Kim slowly opened her eyes.

"Well, because I was the one who had found him and had helped my mother heal him, he had given me his family ring as a gift." Kim lifted her arm and showed the bracelet-ring.

"I have seen you wear this. You never take it off. I thought it was a gift from Luther."

"I am to send it to Jahaziel if ever I am in trouble, and in need of his help. I did send the ring to him once, when I came upon Queen Joyce before the birth of Princess Teri. Jahaziel was good to his word, and came quickly."

"I see. Do you think I would be jealous of Sir Jahaziel?"

Huw asked her.

Surprise registered on Kim's face as her eyes opened wide.

"You are not jealous?"

"No. Why should I be? You belong to me, and I to you."

"Jahaziel's jealous of you."

"Good. Well should he be. I have a forever promise from the most beautiful creature that ever floats and, might I say, walks, this world of fairies and men."

Kim could not stop her tears of relief, and hugged Huw for several long moments. When she started to hiccup, he opened the letter and read aloud.

Kim, gold fairy princess and Huw, fey guard and harp maker,

I wish you all the best in your life together. May you have many happy memories for years to come, and always be surprised by each other in the best of ways. Knowing Kim as I do, I think that will be a common occurrence.

Please accept my gift of congratulations. Find Luther, he will show it to you. I hope you like it, and that it serves you both well in your years ahead.

Your friend,

Jahaziel Miguel Carlos Fuentes, first knight and loyal servant of King Crawford

They jumped up together and flew, laughing, running and grabbing at each other in search of Luther.

"Father, Mother. Where are you taking us?"

"You never were one for patience Kim. It is not far now," Glenlillian said, while she and Luther held hands as they slowly glided ahead.

Huw and Kim followed behind them, and they spoke softly to one another, trying to guess what kind of gift could be hiding in the woods. As they approached a clearing, the gift came into full view.

Luther smiled brightly, and knew that Jahaziel's gift had just the effect he had wanted. The house was beautiful. The roof was not thatched, but had hundreds of square wooden blocks covering it. The blocks shone in the glow of the setting sun from pine tree sap lavishly spread to protect the roof from the weather.

The covered porch went from one end to the other, and the front door had two huge, double shutters on either side. The ornate latches and hooks held the shutters open for the house to receive as much sun as possible. When shut, they protected the inside from storms, wind, and hail.

Glenlillian and Kim flew inside to discover all the treasures there. And the squeals of laughter from the women told Luther and Huw they were going to be there for a long time.

"Have a seat, Huw." Luther pointed to one of the four chairs set on the porch that were clearly there for relaxation, and to enjoy the view.

"I will go and fetch us some of Glenlillian's special brew. She dropped it by earlier knowing we men would be thirsty after such a long travel," Luther said. When he came back holding two clay cups, he handed Huw one and sat in the chair next to his newly acquired son.

"How did Jahaziel do this with such secrecy, Luther?"

"He had help from some of our clan as well as King Crawford's craftsman. I was as surprised as you are now when he approached me about the idea. He had drawings, and I could not help myself. I decided to like the fellow."

There they sat, fey king and first guard, enjoying the sounds of the women talking, laughing and giggling inside the newly built home.

Chapter Twelve

Arnault stumbled once again as he wandered aimlessly through the dark, Haunted Forest.

His escape was difficult, and long in the planning, but he managed to get the key to his cell when he persuaded a greedy guard he would make him rich beyond measure.

Once they had cleared the wooded area of Fitzhuwlyn Castle, he had killed the guard. Assured he would not be followed he had headed for the magical land of Newry.

Speaking to himself, he complained, "They think I am afraid. I will show all of them. I know where the end of this forest leads. I know where the beautiful land of Newry is. I will claim it for my own once again. Had I known to gather just a few more men, I would not have lost that battle. What business is it of William's to protect such a land? He has no true claim there. Crawford had no business giving that land to his wife's cousin. William did nothing to deserve it. It should have been given to me for my humiliation those many years ago—payment for injuries inflicted upon me in that joust.

"No, no. I will seize it all, and no one will take it from me. I have men still loyal to me. When I am strong again, I will crush Crawford, William and Gauwain. But I will save my temper for Jahaziel. I will torture him for long days, and he will beg me for mercy. Yes, yes. He will beg me for mercy, and I will not give it!"

His loud voice echoed through the forest, awakening the creatures within.

The ear-piercing scream bounced off the trees. Arnault ran wildly, searching for a place to hide. Falling forward, he rolled down a small hill, and then quickly jumped back up. He looked behind him as he continued to run.

The screaming creature was closing in on him fast. He stumbled for the last time, and was relieved to see the cave up ahead. He ran blindly into the sanctuary, unaware of his fate.

Screaming Mirrorme stopped short of the cave entrance. She knew what lay within its darkness. The blood-curdling scream from the man told her the creature had found him. She turned around, and walked back to her home, upset she had not gotten to him first, for she was very hungry.

Sixty moons had passed since the acceptance ceremony of Kim and Huw.

Now, in the silence of the garden, a full winter solstice moon glowed upon the nine fully developed pods of the Concordia plant. It was nearly time for the birthing of fairies.

Kim and her husband Huw smiled at Kim's parents, who were joyful in the knowledge that they would be present to witness history being made.

The smallest of the pods began to move first, and Kim and Glenlillian seemed to hold their breath as they knelt at the base of this large, unopened flower. Then, the fairy mist began to fall, and the dew awakened the first of the babies.

"I am not ready. I cannot do this." Kim looked at her mother with her eyes wide with concern.

"Kim, we are all here for you. You can do this. Hush now, and prepare to hold your firstborn," her mother said.

Tears of joy ran down Kim's face as the first pod bloomed, opening its flower to expel the fairy baby and receive the nourishing mist. Kim gathered the first of nine tiny blankets given to her by Glenlillian. And, with gentle care, she held her fairy baby, wrapping her in the warm blanket. Not far from the garden, the sound of quiet singing could be heard as several fairies from the clan sang the fairy birthing song.

Kim handed the first of the nine to Huw, who was awestruck. With shaking hands he received his little fairy with a welcoming kiss. Luther looked over Huw's shoulder, and neither fey could speak from the wonder of it all.

Then Kim and Glenlillian scooted to the next pod and repeated their movements until all nine fairies were born.

Kim, Huw and Glenlillian held two fairy babies each, and Luther held three. The singing continued as they were serenaded by the fairies of the clan to the home of Kim and Huw. They moved with graceful splendor as each held the babies close to their hearts.

When the fairy babies were gently placed, one next to the other, in the large wooden cradle handcrafted by their father, all four stood together in quiet amazement at the sight before them.

"Kim, I have brought the first feeding of the nourishing nectar from the Concordia plant," Glenlillian said. "We will need to milk more tomorrow, but there is plenty for now. Let them sleep while they can. But prepare yourselves. When they awake, your life and Huw's will never be the same."

Kim smiled at her mother and agreed, indeed, they would not.

Satisfied that Kim and Huw would be fine for the evening, Luther and Glenlillian kissed them both and floated to the door.

Luther turned and spoke to Huw. "I expect to see you tomorrow, Huw. I have some new feys who wish to become guards, and I need you to observe them while they train."

"I will be there at first light, Luther."

As they stopped at the door, Luther and Glenlillian turned to Kim and said together, "Kim, gold fairy mother, be well."

"I cannot believe they are all finally asleep, Huw. I am exhausted."

"I am as well."

Kim smiled as she leaned back in her chair and closed her eyes. Her hair moved playfully, as a soft and gentle breeze blew through the abundant trees near their home.

"It is a good thing that I am promised to the only harp maker in three clans, and extremely grateful that our little moonkins love that sound. I do not know what we would have done if not for that magical harp of yours."

"When I was young, other feys would laugh at me when I began my search for materials to build a harp that I had imagined many times. Yet I did not have the courage to tell my father that was what I wanted to do," Huw said.

He turned his head and smiled at Kim. "I knew that I could create something magical, with beauty as well as function. But never could I have imagined in one thousand passings of the moon that I would create something that would save my life."

Kim quickly covered her mouth so she would not laugh out loud, risking waking their nine sleeping fairy babies. She waved a hand, and pleaded for him to stop.

Before she could speak again, Kim turned toward a thickly wooded area just shy of their porch, and announced, "King Halcort comes."

Halcort, king of all the deer of all the lands, stood tall and majestic next to the wild rose bushes Sir Jahaziel had planted, himself, just a few moons ago. Their scent rose with the breeze, and Halcort lifted his head with appreciation, and took a long, lovely sniff.

"These roses are splendid, Kim. Did you and Huw plant them?"

"No, Your Majesty, a good friend of ours did. It was a gift to us after the birth of our daughters. Nine different species of roses were hand-picked and planted by him."

"Do you speak of Sir Jahaziel?"

"Yes," Kim answered. "You know Sir Jahaziel?"

"I make it my business to know things that concern all of us who share these meadows, woods, forests and the waters of the sea. However, I have not personally met the human. Is he a good human, Kim?"

"Yes, he is, Halcort. And Kim and I both trust him," Huw said with confidence.

"As you can see by looking at me, I have brought you a few gifts. If you would not mind, could you untie this rope and remove the sack attached to it? This will relieve me of the promise of delivery. You can open it now or later, whatever your choice."

Kim's eyes sparkled with unshed tears as she tried to imagine what the gifts could be, and who might have sent them.

"I see you are both surprised, so I will tell you they come from…wait, let me find his words…your elf. Yes, yes. Your elf."

Huw's eyebrows rose, and he questioned Kim, "You own an elf?"

They all burst out laughing, and Halcort nodded his yes to Kim's question of something to eat and drink.

"Your hay is especially sweet, Kim, and quite filling. I thank you for your kindness, but I must return to my family. They are always nervous when I am away, even if it is only for short moments."

"Thank you for your thoughtfulness in bringing these gifts, Your Majesty," Huw said. "Please tell Kim's elf we are most pleased, and thankful for the gifts."

Huw smiled warmly. "Let me walk with you a way. I must take a trip to the gardens of the Concordia's and bring fresh nectar for my little ones' next feeding. I am afraid the plants no longer enjoy our visits, and seem to shake in fear at our approach."

They laughed together, and the great deer and fey guard stayed close as they spoke of things of concern, enjoying the last of the sun's warm light.

Kim tried to wait for Huw, but she could not. She fussed with the knotted sack until it gave way and, with greedy, yet gentle, hands, she spread everything onto the porch in front of her.

Her breath caught in her throat, and tears ran down her face as she looked upon the colorful array of clothing. Nine tiny dresses of exact size and shape lay before her. Clearly sewn on the front, upper-right corner of each dress was an intricate design of a small animal of the forest, cleverly arranged with beads that glittered and twinkled.

Kim needed to bring them close to her face in order to be able to see what they were, and she smiled in wonder at the tiny Guinea pig, chipmunk, mole, mouse, hamster, gerbil, shrew, gecko, and chameleon.

Lifting each dress, one at a time, she spoke with breathless words the poems tied to each dress sleeve with morning glory twine.

"Blue is the sky, seen on days crystal clear. May baby one wear it happily, and not shed one tear.

"Green is the grass, sweet and fine. May baby two wear it

happily, born to you just in time.

"Pink is the night sky, yawning for to sleep. May baby three wear it happily, a precious jewel that you keep.

"Orange is the boldness of flowers that shine. May baby four wear it happily, she is truly one-of-a-kind.

"Purple's wild heather grows even in the cold. May baby five wear it happily, no sweeter gift for you to hold.

"White is the sky's fluffy clouds on days fair. May baby six wear it happily, held often with gentle care.

"Brown is the earth, rich and strong. May baby seven wear it happily, through winter months that are long.

"Yellow are the daisies, filled with laughter quite merry. May baby eight wear it happily, and grow to be a great fairy.

"Red is the boldness of a stormy night sky. May baby nine wear it happily, with great speed she will fly."

Kim opened the folded parchment paper and read the note written in bold script.

> *Kim. I hope you are happy with my gifts to your little ones. They are made with the application of elvin magic. Each garment will grow as they grow. They will never hold a stain nor soaking rain, and will un-crumple when laid flat.*
>
> *I bid you great happiness to you and your new family.*
>
> *Egwin*

Kim did not hear Huw's approach, and he lovingly looked down at his promised. Her tears ran freely and unabashedly down her face, and her smile showed her joy and beauty.

"My sweet golden fairy, why do you cry?"

"Look, Huw, fairy baby dresses."

And so the nine fairy babies grew in strength and size.

They loved everything around them as well as their parents, grandparents, creatures of the forest, food, walking plants, bees, hummingbirds, and most especially each other. But what they loved best of all, were the color of their magic dresses.

PART TWO

Princess Teri and the Nine Fairies

Chapter Thirteen

Long ago, in a land no longer remembered, there was a princess named Teri, who lived in the most beautiful castle in the land. Her parents were King Crawford and Queen Joyce. The king and queen loved Princess Teri very much, and doted on her every whim, often bringing her gifts from their many travels. It saddened them deeply that they could not take the young princess with them when they attended to their royal duties outside the castle.

Alas, all the royal physicians agreed that the princess could not survive outside. Poor Princess Teri was allergic to grass, flowers, dirt, mud, bugs, dust, rain, the sun, leaves, rocks, the river, wind, ants, mushrooms that grew wild, and the sky. This filled her with great sadness, as she longed for a chance to play outside in the woods near her castle.

~

Princess Teri sat atop her mother's bed watching her pack for yet another royal trip, silently wondering how many more places her parents would go without her.

Queen Joyce walked to where the princess sat smiling. She brushed her daughter's hair back from her face, and wondered how her child had come upon such light red hair, those huge green eyes, and pale skin. Her own dark hair, eyes and skin resembled that of her husband's, and most of their family members.

She kissed her on the cheek, and spoke to her on the subject of her allergies. "The physicians did mention to me there is a good possibility that you could outgrow all of your allergies, perhaps as soon as your birthday. Just imagine all of us enjoying the celebration, coming up just a few months from now, watching you play outside. Eleven could be the magic number."

"Have a little more patience, sweetheart. I am confident the physicians are truthful in their assessment of your coming good health," Teri's mother said.

That evening, while she whispered her bedtime prayers, the princess remembered her mother's words of hope. She did not want to be disappointed if what the physicians had said did not come true, so she quickly added, "Perhaps a few new friends to play with would help with the loneliness, and that would be enough."

Off in the distant darkness, the sound of the child's praying could be heard echoing through the forest. Nine fairy sisters flitted toward the sound, waving their golden wings slowly back and forth. They suspended their movements and, upon hearing the softly spoken request, all nine decided to be the princess's friend.

Each fairy had a favorite color, and wore only that color—so much so that it became her identity. Purple Fairy, Orange Fairy, Green Fairy, Blue Fairy, Pink Fairy, Red Fairy, Yellow Fairy, Brown Fairy, and White Fairy were quite pleased with their colorful choices in clothing.

"OK, we are all in agreement to be friends with the girl in the big castle," Pink Fairy said, as she smiled at her sisters.

"I did not say I agree just yet," Brown Fairy stated. "Are you sure we will not get into trouble?"

"Ah, did we all have a brain sneeze and forget about Mama telling us, on more than one occasion that we are not to have contact with people?" Purple Fairy uttered.

Hysterical laughter broke out among the girls, and they fell to the ground, trying to catch their breath.

Green Fairy wiped her eyes, then sat up and spoke boldly, "Oh, yes. I remember. But she is a girl, not a people yet."

White Fairy, scrunched up her nose and eyes, then said, "That does not seem entirely correct. Our thinking is off here."

"We are not even supposed to be here, at this end of our woods," Yellow Fairy reminded them.

Blue Fairy flitted into the center of the group. "No, no. I remember. Mama said not to go near the meadow or the castle. She did not say we could not be here at the edge of our woods."

With her hand on her hips, Orange Fairy said in a haughty voice, "And how do you think we will get to the girl without going past the meadow and into the castle?"

The sisters turned and look at White Fairy.

"No way are you going to talk me into taking us through the wrinkle. What happens if we get caught?" White Fairy asked.

"Please, White. We will be your lookouts while you snoop." All the sisters nodded their heads as Blue Fairy continued, "You and Orange are the best snoopers. We will not tell a soul."

"Our lips are sealed," they said in unison.

"You know I always get a headache when I go through the wrinkle, and Orange does too when she goes invisible."

Red Fairy came forward, and said, "And I always take your headaches away."

"I will not do this until we make the promise. Then we can come back just before sunrise, after our chores," White Fairy bargained.

She held out her hands to her sisters. Then White Fairy began to move them into the promise circle—a circle they formed when they first realized they could hover. With their pinky fingers locked, they remained suspended, close to the ground, and began the slow rotation.

Here, within the circle, all secrets between them were safe, and decisions made were not spoken of again unless the need arose. The quiet sound of their secret words filled the forest with the music of chanting.

"Mother, I think the Concordia pods are fine. I see no problems here. Did you bring the moss dust?" Kim asked.

"Yes, I also brought crushed hyacinth blooms," her mother answered. "I've been experimenting with soaking the blooms in water, then setting them in the sun. Once the sun dries them, I crush them with my mixing stone. After I pound them into a fine powder, I slowly add the bog moss, crushed sea shells, and the ash from burnt oak. Fallen tree branches have been so abundant lately I have had no trouble finding them.

"After burning and cooling them, I add their ash to the rest of the mixture. I have made enough soil-enriching compound to last through the coming fall days ahead."

Glenlillian handed Kim a small sack of the dried mixture, and she watched her mother sprinkle it around the base of several Concordia plants. She urged Kim to do the same on the other side of the garden.

When they finished the task of caretakers, Glenlillian decided this was the perfect time to ask Kim to come with her.

"Would you like to go with me to Coremerick, Kim? I was asked to come and assess their Concordia garden, and to stay for a visit. Perhaps I could throw around a bit of my soil-enriching compound, just for effect. The clan of Coremerick's caretakers worry needlessly. And, can you believe, they actually had a vote to bid me come?"

"I did not know this," Kim answered. "You tell me very little these days, Mother, and I worry when you travel so far alone. Can you not wait until father returns?"

"Kim, Sweetling, you are always so very busy now that you are a mother, and your duties have seemed to increase since becoming gold fairy. I would wait for Luther's return, but they have summoned me to come now. You know the clan would love to see all of my grandfairies. You are especially welcome, as well, as you are the talk of all the clans since their births. It would be a lovely trip and visit for all of us."

"Yes, I agree. But as you say, my duties have increased, and I too have been asked to come by and check on a few things within our clan. Apparently, a few young feys have gone missing, and I need to focus with a little quiet time to myself in order to seek them out. I plan on giving them a good dressing down when I find them, for giving everyone such a scare."

"I understand, Kim. Please tell your father where I have gone. And ask him whether he wouldn't mind stopping by Coremerick to collect me. Otherwise, they will try to keep me there longer than I would like."

"Were you not just there, Mother? I thought I heard you speaking to Green about Karyn's newly discovered calming plant?"

"No, no. That was Karapalis. And Kareen is the only Concordia caretaker left since the passing of Alowishises. They had a real problem with that garden, and I spent nearly one passing of a moon there. But Kareen showed me the new calming plant and how she dried and mixed it into one of her famous teas. That tea smelled divine, and tasted like honey and blueberries. The poor dear; I think she is lonely, and no one in her clan seems to be interested in her abilities or her discoveries. I felt very privileged to have received such a wonderful gift, and I must say it truly works."

Kim laughed heartily, and said, "Mother, you and your recipes."

As she hugged her daughter, Glenlillian smiled, and said, "Be sure to call on the rain on your way home, Kim. Not a deluge, just a slow constant drizzle should do."

"Oh, Mother. I almost forgot. Could you stop by your favorite garden and forage for a few eye and muscle healing herbs? I believe we are running a little low on those particular plants."

She nodded to her daughter, and they went their separate ways.

"And where do you think you are all going so early this morning?" Kim said when she saw the guilty looks on her daughter's faces as they tried to sneak out without her notice. She waited for them to answer.

Orange Fairy spoke with confidence, "Since we are done with our chores, we decided to search for good stuff to make a surprise for father."

"Yes, but we do not know, just yet, what it will be," White Fairy said with a rush of words.

"Mama, are you sure he will be home in a few days?" questioned Blue Fairy.

Kim smiled. "That is a very sweet idea and, no matter what you can come up with, I am sure he will be very surprised. And yes, he and your grandfather will be back very soon," Kim answered her.

Her daughters hurriedly flew out their door in fits of laughter, giggles, hushed words, hugs and kisses, hair pulling and screams. The sounds of pure joy following in their wake.

As the sun began its slow climb into morning, Princess Teri awoke to the sound of buzzing in her ears. She sat up quickly, opened her eyes, and discovered the buzzing sound was coming from the wings of nine little, smiling fairies. It looked to her like a rainbow shining in front of her face and around her head.

At first, the princess thought she might still be dreaming, so she rubbed her eyes with her hands. Then she looked again, and said, "Yep, still there."

Then another sound came, the sound of voices, quietly speaking in a sudden rush, like soft winds blowing through forest trees, getting louder and louder. The fairies saw that the princess was awake, and started talking excitedly to her all at once.

The laughing princess spoke, "Please, I cannot understand one word. Shall we take turns? I will ask each of you a question, and you can ask me a question."

All the fairies agreed and, one by one, they sat themselves at the foot end of her bed.

"May I go first?" asked the princess.

All the fairies said "yes" together, while vigorously nodding their heads.

"Where did all of you come from?"

Blue Fairy gracefully glided forward, and spoke in a surprisingly low voice.

"I am Blue Fairy," she said, pointing to herself. "My sisters and I came from the forest just beyond the woods, not far from your castle. We heard your prayer, and we all decided to be your friend."

Just then, Purple Fairy jumped up and blurted out, "This is wonderful. My sister fairies and I have been waiting for a chance to be friends with people. We play in the forest with bunches of bears, cooters, deer…"

Quickly, Pink Fairy put her hand over Purple Fairy's mouth and said, "Please forgive my sister, but she can go on and on until she names every animal in our forest."

There was complete silence for a moment, and then everyone started laughing. They chatted with one another for an hour, and asked many questions while getting to know each other.

"Well, are we ready to go outside?" Pink Fairy asked. "We can show you all the different places we play, and where we live." When Pink Fairy suddenly stopped talking, all the fairies saw the princess shake her head back and forth.

White Fairy came forward, and questioned, "Why ever not? Are you a prisoner?"

"Well, not exactly," said the princess. "I cannot venture outside. I am allergic to everything, and will become very ill if I do. My poor parents worry much over this difficulty."

The fairies looked at her in stunned silence. Then all at once, they spoke to each other with rushed words, pointing fingers, shaking heads, and flapping wings.

At last, they turned to the princess, and Green Fairy finally spoke, "All of us, upon our births, were granted magical gifts. Because we all agreed to be your friend, we wish to use our gifts to help you."

The princess had no idea what the fairies were talking about, and she let them know.

Green Fairy pulled something out of her pocket, and held out her left hand and continued, "We can use our magic to sprinkle on this herb. You eat one a day, and it will help with all your allergies. But only if you want this."

Orange Fairy pulled at Green Fairy's dress and spoke,

"What else do you have in those pockets, Green? Are my missing hair ribbons in there?"

Green Fairy slapped at her sister's hands, and laughed.

Giggling at the antics of the fairies, the princess finally answered excitedly, "Oh yes, please. I often dream what it would be like to go outside—to see the sky and pet my rabbit, Bun Bun Bunny."

So all the fairies collected a handful of their fairy dust and, one by one, they whispered in their ancient language, and sprinkled the herb. Then, with the magic herb ready, Green Fairy handed it to the princess to eat.

"I have to sit down, I feel a little dizzy."

While the princess sat, the fairies continued to speak to each other quietly.

"Well, how do you feel?" asked Brown Fairy.

"I feel much better thank you," answered the princess.

"Excellent. Now we can go play outside," shouted all the fairies at once.

In a rush of colors and giggles, the princess and the fairies bounded toward her bedroom door. The princess reached her door first, and then realized she was not dressed properly. So she quickly turned around to tell them, which caused all the fairies to slam into her.

The princess sprang into action by picking up her nightgown at the hem, and lifted it up just in time to catch all the fairies. The fairies bounced up and down, and slammed their heads and bodies together. They began hollering different things.

"Whoa, Nellie."

"Bounce-um, trounce-um."

"Save me, Mona."

"Give a girl a break."

"Watch my hair."

"Madre De Hadas."

"Ya think."

"Oh, you are not on my dress."

"Help."

Princess Teri laughed so hard she had tears running down her face. She slid slowly to the floor with her treasures tucked tenderly into her nightgown. She finally stopped laughing, and very carefully checked each fairy for damage.

She touched them gently, one at a time, and did not sense something special had passed between them. The fairy sisters did, however, and they knew it was a significant moment.

This was the first time the princess noticed the slight differences between the fairies. Although their facial features were exact, two of the fairies had white/blonde-colored hair, while the others had every shade of blonde in between. They also ranged from the darkest of skin color to the lightest. And Green Fairy had the most wonderful assortment of freckles she had ever seen.

Their eyes, however, stood out the most. Blue Fairy's eyes were so light blue they seemed white. White Fairy's eyes were periwinkle blue. Purple, Brown, and Orange fairies had black eyes. Yellow's eyes were hazel, and Red's were amber. Green's were pale green, and Pink Fairy's eyes were a light shade of purple. They all appeared to be the same age, and the princess wondered how that was possible, as her mind questioned the nature of their births.

Satisfied that they were all fine, she finally said, "The king and queen are not here, so I was thinking that I could write them a short message telling them that I am fine with going out-of-doors, and that I have found an herb that helps quiet my allergies. Also, I should write where I will be, just in case they return before I do.

Let me dress quickly, and I will do just that."

"That is a great idea," they said in unison as if one fairy spoke.

"Our cook, Mrs. Baker, needs to know as well. She will not let me leave otherwise, and I could end up going to bed without my supper." The princess said this with great gusto.

All this was done, and the princess continued speaking to them while they walked out into the courtyard. They headed to the royal animal hut to pick up Bun Bun Bunny, knowing he would enjoy the day just as much as they would.

Off they went, laughing, running, and flying toward the meadow near the woods, just behind the castle.

Chapter Fourteen

Agnes, once a beautiful lady-in-waiting to the queen, had become an angry, jealous, evil woman. Her long, brown hair had lost its color, and she seemed to be a little shorter these days. As she ventured out in search of herbs, she could hear laughter echoing through the woods near her cottage.

Instantly, she recognized Princess Teri's voice, and memories of her past filled her mind. Agnes closed her eyes, drifting back to the day of her banishment. That day came shortly after the birth of the princess, and bitter memories came rushing forward like an angry, swollen river after a storm.

Agnes snapped back to the present. Her once-lovely face, now ugly with anger, broke into a smile at the thought of sweet revenge.

This day Agnes would remember as a great day of triumph, and the plan to kidnap the princess began.

Ever so slowly, she walked closer to the sound of singing and laughter. She peeked through a thicket at the very edge of the meadow, and she could not believe what she saw. It was Princess Teri with the sister fairies. *No,* she thought angrily, *this cannot be*. Her mind raced with questions. How was she ever going to get the fairies away from the princess? What would she do with the princess once she had her, and where would she put her?

Perhaps creating a large inescapable cage and putting it outside her cottage against a wall would be most ideal. *Oh yes,* she pondered, *this is a very good idea.* Agnes knew she would have to move quickly.

Princess Teri was overwhelmed with her surroundings. She touched everything within reach. Tears of joy ran down her face as she collected flowers from the meadow. The grass smelled heavenly, reminding her of the exact day she was told she could no longer venture outside.

~

"Princess, you were told several times not to roll in the grass," Miss Maggie admonished Princess Teri. "Look at you, covered with hives. Now we must add grass to the long list of your allergies. Your mother will be angry with me for letting you out with Christopher and Myles for so long. That Myles is a handsome devil, and I know you have feelings for each other. But I should not have let him persuade me to let you out-of-doors. Stop fussing now, and let me put this pig fat on you."

"No, it smells awful, Miss Maggie, and it does not help."

"Mrs. Smith has assured me it works. You need to leave it on longer, give it time to work."

"No. Does Mrs. Smith have anything else besides pig fat?"

"Let me go ask her. I will be right back, and do not go below stairs until I return."

Princess Teri heard pebbles hitting the half-open shutters of the only opening in the south-facing wall of her room. She walked to the sound of voices that were calling her name. She pushed the shutters wide, and leaned out. She laughed as she observed her friends pretending to beat one another—flexing their muscles, dancing with invisible women, and spouting poetry.

When Myles saw her red face, he stopped Christopher with a raised hand, walked closer, and looked up. He spoke with concern in his voice. "Teri, I am sorry you suffer again. We did not know the grass would cover you with hives. You must listen to your parents and stay inside. You seem to accumulate more allergies with each passing day, and you must understand the danger to your health if you leave your castle. Christopher and I will visit you as often as we are able. We can bring you whatever you need while we are out and about."

Christopher nodded his head in agreement.

"Is there anything you would like us to fetch you?" When her coughing began, Myles and Christopher went into the castle to fetch Mrs. Smith. Her chamomile and herbal teas were quite famous for their medicinal qualities, and were the only remedy for the princess's coughing fits.

The sound of the fairies laughing brought the princess back to the present, and away from her sad past.

"Oh, my dear new friends." spoke the princess. "I have had such a wonderful time playing with all of you, but I think it is time to return to the castle. I am a little hungry, and I know Bun Bun Bunny is, too. How about you? Do you eat food?"

"Of course, we do," said Orange Fairy confused. "We eat mostly berries, grapes, kiwi, melons, and bunches of vegetables. You know, stuff like that. But Red Fairy's favorite is avocados. Mama mixes them up special, and calls it gukasmasholie, and it tastes divine."

The princess smiled brightly at thought of the fairies mother.

"What is your mother's name?"

The fairies looked sheepish, and did not answer the princess.

"I promise not to tell. But if it is a secret, I have no need to know."

She paused a moment, then continued, "Are all of you allowed to be here with me? Do you have permission from your mother?"

Since White Fairy seemed to be the spokesfairy for her sisters, she chose her words carefully. "No princess. We are not allowed to be here. We are not allowed to talk with, or be seen by, people. But since you are not a people yet, our curiosity got the better of us. Besides, are you not glad we came? Are you not outside because of us?"

Princess Teri could not help smiling, and realized these nine fairy sisters were very brave to disobey their mother, risking possible punishment just to be with her.

"Yes, I am very happy to be out-of-doors once again. And since I gave nothing away in my message about fairies coming to my rescue, I will keep your secret." The princess did not have the heart to tell them she was, in fact, a people.

"We should start collecting fruits and vegetables to take back just in case Mama asks us where we have been," Yellow Fairy stated.

"Could we all stop thinking about our stomachs and start heading back to the castle?" said Red Fairy. And, as she floated closer to the princess, she asked, "Do you think we can all come back tomorrow?"

"I would love to come back here tomorrow and be with all of you again," she answered. She bent down, and picked up Bun Bun Bunny for their journey back.

"I cannot wait for Myles and Christopher to see me out here. They will be very happy for me," she told Red Fairy.

Pink Fairy floated forward, and asked, "Who are Myles and Christopher?"

"Myles is Scott Albright's son. Mr. Albright is our

blacksmith. And Christopher's father, Thomas Fontaine, is our main builder."

"Are you promised to Myles and Christopher?" Green Fairy questioned.

"No." she smiled at the thought of an engagement to both of them. "We three are great friends, but I have always been much closer to Myles. My hope is that we would marry one day."

"I will grow you beautiful flowers and bring them to your ceremony," Green Fairy announced boldly.

"That would be lovely, Green Fairy, and I invite all of you when that time comes. But Myles has to ask me first," she said, beaming.

Purple Fairy moved closer to the princess, and asked, "Why do people have two names? Do you have two names like Christopher and Myles? We fairies have one name and try not to repeat names because that would get really confusing and…"

"Stop talking, Purple, and let her answer your question," Orange Fairy said. She laughed, and smiled at the princess.

"Fitzhuwlyn is my last name, but I have more."

"More names?" they all whispered.

"Yes. Would you like to hear them?"

They nodded in unison.

"Teri is a short version of my first name, Terricethea. I am told it was my great-grandmother's first name. I am called Terricethea Jasmine Gwendolyn Doreen Murphy Allen Fitzhuwlyn."

"Wow," they whispered.

It did not go unnoticed by the princess how the fairies constantly touched each other in loving gestures of kissing, hugging, holding hands, and constantly fussing with each other's hair. The princess's mind raced with an idea about what it would be like to have brothers or sisters—siblings she could be with, and share her life with. She also wondered if it was too late for her mother to have more children.

She cleared her mind, and then took one last look around. She took a deep breath of clean, fresh air without so much as a cough or sneeze and, in her very regal manner, said, "Come."

Agnes continued to listen to the cheerful laughter and happy singing as it faded into the distance. She smiled as she got closer to her cottage. With every step she took, the plan formed most perfectly in her mind, and she knew exactly how she would kidnap the princess and make her a slave.

She would use her to get everything she wanted from the king and queen. She spoke quietly to herself, and uttered, "She will do everything I say. I will starve her so she is too weak to cry out for help, or to argue."

Her evil, low laughter was not heard by anyone or any creature, except for Agnes herself.

As night began to turn into day, the fairies sat in the meeting meadow discussing their project. Red Fairy leaned close to Brown Fairy and asked, "What is that?"

"I have no idea."

"Was it not Orange's idea to tell Mama we were making something for father upon his return?" asked White Fairy.

"Yes. And if we do not come up with something quick, Mama will be suspect of us."

"That is suspicious, Pink, not suspect."

"You think you know everything, Blue. I think you should make father's gift." Brown Fairy stopped working on the surprise and looked to all of her sisters for help.

White Fairy closed her eyes, and went to her inside place. Then she spoke in a soft whisper, and uttered, “Father loves his harps, and needs new things to make another. I see a place at the edge of the ocean that washes up a strange-looking wood. We will find what we need there.”

“Wow. That was different,” Yellow Fairy stated.

“Hey! The edge of the ocean is not too far from the castle. When we visit the princess we can look for the wood after. What do you think?” Pink Fairy questioned.

All the fairies agreed, and off they went to plan their next visit to the princess. To make sure they would remember to search for the strange wood, they sang their special song. Like a game, they took turns in the chanting—twirling in circles, gently touching and smiling.

“I will remind you, Orange.”

“I will remind you, Purple.”

“I will remind you, Pink.”

“I will remind you, White.”

“I will remind you, Brown.”

“I will remind you, Red.”

“I will remind you, Yellow.”

“I will remind you, Blue.”

“And, I will remind you, Green,” Blue Fairy finished.

Princess Teri awoke slowly the next morning, and felt a tickling sensation on her nose. She opened her eyes, crossed them, and saw Green Fairy brushing her wings back and forth just at the tip of her nose. Before the princess could help herself, she sneezed, and sent the fairy flying across the room, where she landed in an open box of white face powder. For a moment, no one said a word until the fairy climbed out of the box covered in the powder from head to toe, and wing to wing.

Everyone in the princess's room laughed hysterically at seeing the powder-covered fairy. Poor Green Fairy started coughing and coughing, sending little bits of powder from her mouth everywhere. The princess felt pity for the fairy, and she got out of her bed and walked over to her dressing table. She gently picked up the fairy, placed her in her hand, and dusted her off with the sleeve of her nightgown.

Once the princess could see a little bit of the fairy's face, she spoke in a gentle voice, "Are you all right?"

"Yes," squeaked Green Fairy. As she shook her head from side-to-side, powder fell off her tiny body.

"I hope everyone is still interested in playing outside," announced Blue Fairy quite loudly.

"Yes," they all shouted, including Green Fairy, who sounded more like a frog than a fairy. While the princess dressed, she chatted with the fairies, and told them about her dream that night. She hoped they could tell her what it meant.

"I was in our meadow alone looking for something, and could hear thunder in the distance, so I started running for home. I was nearly out of breath, and had to stop, when I realized I was still in the meadow."

All the fairies sat on a single window ledge in Princess Teri's room, and they listened with great interest.

"What do you think it means?" asked the princess as she finished dressing.

"Well," said White Fairy. "I think it means that you are going to be in some kind of danger. I think going outside today is not a good idea.

"What?" shouted Brown Fairy? "You have got to be joking? It was just a dream. I put no stock in spooky dreams. I say we go play outside as planned."

"Brown Fairy is right," stated Pink Fairy. "I think we can handle most anything that comes up. Besides, we are fairies, aren't we? We have enough magic between us to deal with surprises."

At Princess Teri's nod of agreement, the fairies flew toward the door, stopping just inches from it. While eating her magic herb, a quick smile came to the princess's face as she walked out, with the fairies floating cautiously behind her.

Meanwhile, Agnes had spent the entire night in her herb room mixing her potion. Satisfied with the results, she had held up the morsel in her fingers toward a window that faced the rising sun. With squinting eyes, she looked to see if she had left anything of importance out of the recipe.

"Perfection," she said out loud. "That bunny will eat this morsel disguised as a plain, sweet, flower with no problem."

Agnes walked to the wall where her cape hung on a peg, and put it over her shoulders. Her sensitivity to the cold increased each year, and the rain made her bones ache. The sweet and kind disposition she'd had as a child, as told to her by her parents, who have been gone many years now, was no longer evident in the woman she had become. Nothing seemed to make her happy—until now.

With the hood hiding her face, she placed the plain, sweet flower into a pocket, opened the front door, stepped out onto the path that lead to the meadow, and smiled. She walked confidently toward the sound of laughter and voices, and thought to herself that she was the smartest woman ever.

Agnes got close enough to see the bunny off by himself chewing on a tender leaf. She walked ever-so-slowly, ever-so-quietly, until she reached a spot where she could drop the plain, sweet flower. Carefully, she stepped backward to her watching place, and waited.

Bun Bun Bunny hopped around to search for good things to eat. Not far from the princess, he continued smelling, tasting, and touching all the wonderful things around him. *What could this be*, he thought to himself? *Does not look like a leaf, a piece of bark, or, oh, a piece of juicy flower*. Bun Bun Bunny took a good sniff, then decided it smelled good enough to eat. *Not bad*, he reasoned.

He moved away, and searched for more delicious things to eat in the meadow. Poor Bun Bun Bunny did not get very far before he fell into a deep sleep.

Agnes scooped up the bunny, and carried him away without being seen. She reached her cottage quickly, placed the bunny on a bed she had prepared, sat in her rocking chair, and then waited.

Chapter Fifteen

"I think it is time to go back to the castle, princess," Blue Fairy said.

"Yes. I suppose you are right. Perhaps tomorrow I can visit your home. This meadow is huge, but the woods and forest are farther than I expected to walk today."

She looked around, and realized Bun Bun Bunny was nowhere to be seen. She turned from left to right, and looked up and down the meadow. Then she asked, "Has anyone seen Bun Bun Bunny lately?"

"No," all the fairies replied.

"Perhaps we can all search in different directions quickly before it gets dark."

Off everyone went in search of Bun Bun Bunny. With the sound of voices echoing throughout the woods calling out the bunny's name, all were sure he would be found soon.

Princess Teri was getting a little tired, so she sat down on a fallen tree to rest. She wondered where her bunny could be, and then she began smiling. A shadow of bunny ears appeared on the ground just to the princess's left. She turned quickly, and bent down to scoop up the bunny before he could hop off again.

Princess Teri could not utter a scream. The bunny's giant paw quickly covered her mouth, and he lifted her up off the log with the other paw. He took great leaps as he hopped through the woods in the direction of Agnes' cottage.

All the fairies came together in a circle, ringing their tiny hands in frustration. They spoke in rushed words.

"What has become of the princess and her bunny?" Red Fairy whimpered to no one in particular.

"What are we going to do?" Pink Fairy murmured. "It will be dark soon, and we cannot just hover here."

"She could not have gone far. Do you think, Yellow?" Blue Fairy asked.

"I do not know. She was here just a moment ago."

Orange Fairy began to cry, and her sisters hugged her, trying their best to give her comfort.

Green Fairy spoke softly, "It will be OK, Orange, please stop crying."

"I cannot."

"Why?"

"We have lost the princess, and do not have our wood."

White Fairy decided to take charge of the difficult situation and said, "Listen to me. Blue, go fetch Mama. Yellow, I need you to find Princess Teri's friends, Myles and Christopher. Maybe she decided to walk home on her own, and they can look there while we search elsewhere."

"You cannot be serious, White," Pink Fairy nearly shouted. "We cannot risk being seen by anyone else. Mama will punish us good."

"Everything has changed now, Pink. The princess must be found and we need help."

Brown Fairy came forward. "I think we should all go home and tell Mama what has happened. We are all going to be in trouble regardless, so why not ask Mama for help."

"Because," White Fairy exclaimed, "we are running out of time. It is nearly dark now and we can look in more places separately than we can together."

White fairy continued to give orders. "Orange, I need you to find Zoo Zoo Piggy, the guinea pig. If the princess is lost, Zoo Zoo will find her. Green, Pink, Red, Brown, and Purple, keep searching awhile longer. I will stay here just in case the princess comes this way again."

Her sisters nodded their agreement, and did what White Fairy asked.

Touching her wing lights, Pink Fairy glided in the opposite direction. Her concentration was heightened by her ability of awareness. Awareness of her surroundings, like a dog that hunts, made her capable of tracking as well as the guinea pig.

Blue Fairy rushed into her home, and bombarded Kim with the information on everything that had happened. Kim listened quietly to the fear-filled voice of her daughter, and tried not to let her anger or worry show. Being gold fairy mother meant she was an example for her daughters to follow in all situations, and remaining calm was one of many important examples.

When Blue Fairy started to cry, Kim put her arms around her, giving comfort as only a mother could. Then the door flew open again, and in came Brown, Green, Red and Purple fairies.

"Where are White, Yellow, Pink and Orange?" Kim asked, looking at Red Fairy.

"White is still in the woods at the edge of the meadow. Yellow has gone to fetch the princess's friends, Myles and Christopher, and Orange went to speak to Zoo. And I have no idea where Pink is," Red Fairy answered.

Kim spoke in a low voice, "Do you have any idea how very disappointed I am at this moment? You all have broken a trust, and have deliberately deceived me. I see we need to have another discussion about people later. The important thing now is finding the princess as quickly as possible. I need all of you to pay attention to me. This is what we have to do."

They all huddled together as Kim spoke to her very young, frightened daughters.

Yellow Fairy mumbled to herself as she continued her search for Myles and Christopher. "I cannot speak to the boys. What should I say? What will they do to me when they see me? What will I tell White if I cannot find them? I do not know where else to look if they are not at the castle." Yellow Fairy was unaware that Myles and Christopher were on their way to visit Princess Teri at her home at the exact time she continued on her journey toward Fitzhuwlyn Castle. Her fear of meeting them forced upon her by White Fairy intensified. She decided to turn around and go back from whence she came.

Myles and Christopher were excited about their clever plan to coax the princess into venturing out-of-doors. It had been over one week since their last visit. As they took a shortcut through the thickest part of the woods, heading for Fitzhuwlyn Castle, Myles and Christopher spoke quietly to one another. They continued bouncing ideas around on how they might bring Princess Teri outside just long enough to show her Christopher's new gelding.

"We know if she keeps her mouth covered she does not cough overly much, and we could ask her to fetch her mother's cloak as well," Christopher said with confidence.

"Yes, I agree. Oh, do not let me forget to give the cloak a good shake outside before I return it to her. That should throw off dust and any other things that might stick to it. I can hang it on a hook in the entryway for her to use again if our ideas work."

"That is a great plan, Myles. But she cannot pet the gelding—only look. Agreed?"

"Yes, I agree."

"If she thinks these are reasonable ideas, I will go back and fetch the gelding."

In the quickness of one moment, an unexpected thing happened.

The fairy and the boys met eye-to-eye, and the boys stopped their mumblings and movements.

Yellow Fairy, shocked at seeing the boys, and the boys, shocked at seeing a fairy, could neither speak nor seem to breathe. Finally, Yellow Fairy broke the silence.

"I am sorry, I cannot do this," she said, as she slowly glided back away from the boys.

"Wait. Stop. We will not hurt you. Please come back here."

Christopher walked slowly toward the fairy, and Myles followed closely behind.

"Please," Myles whispered.

His soft voice calmed her, and something inside her told her to trust this boy—this Myles. Yellow turned around and floated back, stopping just short of his face.

"You are Myles? Princess Teri's Myles?"

His smile was kind, and his eyes were beautiful, Yellow Fairy thought.

"I am. And this is Christopher."

"Yes. Princess Teri told us about you both. You are really great friends?"

"We are," Christopher assured her.

Myles drew her attention once again with his question. "Who are you, and who are we? Are there more of you here?"

"Before I answer your questions, you must promise not to speak of me or my sisters to any people. Promise, or I will leave this instant."

"We promise," they said in unison.

"I am a fairy, and my name is Yellow. I have eight sisters who are not here at the moment. Do you know of the large castle with the beautiful meadow that sits close to the seashore?"

Their nod signaled her to continue.

"My sister fairies and I were in the woods collecting night flowers for our mother, when we heard a girl praying for a 'few new friends.' We all agreed. Since the girl is not a people yet—we are not allowed to show ourselves to people—we decided to be her friend. Did you know she has a rabbit? She calls him Bun Bun Bunny. That is so cute."

They smiled at each other when the fairy lost her train of thought.

"I am sorry to interrupt you, Yellow Fairy, but we are people." Christopher tried not to laugh, but his smile could not be contained.

"What? Oh no. We have really done it now. We are all going to be in so much trouble," she mumbled.

"What kind of trouble are you all in?" Myles and Christopher spoke at the same time—each thinking what possible trouble could fairies get into. They chuckled, and waited for her to answer.

"Oh, OK. We gave her a magic herb to eat so she could come out and play, and everything was going really well until we lost her bunny, and then we lost her. That is the 'going to be in so much trouble' part."

Christopher coughed, and turned away from the fairy.

"I am sorry. Did I hear you correctly? You lost Princess

Teri?" Myles' strained voice alerted Yellow Fair to his distress, and she did not speak.

As she turned to leave, Yellow Fairy did not realize she had started crying.

"Yellow Fairy, do not leave, and please do not cry. I am as upset at your words as you are in their telling. I must assume you came looking for us, and wish us to join your search."

Yellow Fairy wiped at her eyes, and spoke with a sad voice, "Yes. Oh yes. My sisters sent me to find you and Christopher. Orange Fairy has gone to find a guinea pig we named Zoo Zoo. He knows everything that goes on around here, and is a great tracker."

Her voice shook at her words, and Myles, not wanting to upset her further, smiled as he stated, "Perhaps Zoo Zoo has already found her."

"I certainly hope so. Would you and Christopher come with me to meet my sister, Orange Fairy?"

She smiled at their yes. "Thank you Myles, Christopher."

Pink Fairy put out her wing lights, and put a finger to her mouth, warning Zoo Zoo Piggy not to make a sound.

She peeked slowly around the western corner of a cottage, and saw the princess in the steel cage. Anger came upon her when she heard the soft whimpering that came from the princess.

Pink Fairy's mouth hung open in shock seeing Princess Teri huddled in a far corner, shaking from the cold and rain, and hugging herself in an effort to be warm.

The sound of footsteps stopped the fairy and piggy from going immediately to the princess and, as they receded back into the shadows, they listened to the voice of a woman speaking to the princess.

"My name is Agnes, and I have taken you solely for the purpose of payment—a kidnapping for money, and an unkindness done to me by your parents, returned."

The princess ran to the cage door, and spoke in a shaking voice, "I have done you no harm. If you let me go, I will not tell my parents."

Agnes said not one word and walked back into the cottage, slamming the door behind her.

Princess Teri stopped crying when she saw Pink Fairy slip through the bars of the cage. Without thinking, she grabbed her in a hug and whispered, "I am so glad to see you. Can you get me out of here?"

"No," she said. She removed herself from the princess' arms, and then continued, "I cannot. This cage is made of something I am not familiar with, and it is strong. I promise I will get help quickly. I am sorry I cannot stop this rain, princess. Purple has that gift. The sooner I leave, the sooner I can get you help."

She pointed down to the front of the cage, and finished her words. "This guinea pig will stay with you, and keep an eye on this Agnes. If anything else happens, he will find Orange."

"Please do not leave me, Pink Fairy." Princess Teri started to cry again and it broke Pink Fairy's heart to hear her so distressed.

"Princess, you may call us by our names, and you do not have to say fairy after. We know we are fairies."

When the princess smiled, Pink Fairy knew she had taken her mind off of her troubles, even if it were only for a moment.

"I will be back quickly. You are not alone. Zoo Zoo is here."

She went to the piggy, struggled a moment because of his size and weight, picked him up, went back through the bars, and placed him in Princess Teri's arms.

"He is great company. Are you not, Zoo Zoo?" she crooned.

When she saw the princess smile again, Pink Fairy flew away to get help.

After the initial shock wore off of seeing another fairy, Myles and Christopher could not believe what Orange Fairy was saying.

"I cannot express my sorrow properly and, knowing my sisters and I are the cause of this difficulty, you must understand we have much regret," Orange Fairy explained. "But, before going home, my sister Pink Fairy informed me that a woman named Agnes has taken the princess to her cottage. She is locked in a cage that is out in the open and bolted against a far wall. A guinea pig we call Zoo Zoo is with the princess now and is keeping an eye on that evil woman. He is a good spy, Myles, and he will tell us if anything else happens. Apparently, the princess's bunny is now a giant of a rabbit, and he was the one who put her there by command of this Agnes."

As her last words ended, her tears began. Myles approached her and, with tender words, lifted his hand and wiped her face with a gentle touch. Her look of surprise was equal to Myles', and something he did not understand passed between them.

"Please do not cry, little Orange Fairy. I think if we put our heads together, we can surly come up with a plan to release the princess."

"We realize that all of you are truly upset by the events of this day. I am comforted in the fact that the little piggy is willing to spy on Agnes and watch over the princess. But I wonder if it will be a safe thing for him to do," Christopher questioned.

"Yes, he will be fine. He is a cautious little fellow," she said shyly.

Her thoughts traveled to her sisters, and she wondered if it would help Myles and Christopher to know about the abilities of each fairy. Would she get into trouble if she told?

What if she told him she could become invisible for short bits of time, or that Red could heal anything or anyone, that Purple could change the weather, that Green could grow all things that started from seeds, and was becoming a great herbalist, that Blue's singing could move you to tears as well as move objects, that White could glimpse little bits of the future and could create what she calls a wrinkle that moves her through time, that Pink's wings helped them see in the darkest of nights, and that she was a great tracker, that Brown was the tallest and strongest of them all, or that Yellow had the gift of great kindness and could judge one's character?"

"I think we should try to collect some tools before we speak with White Fairy," Myles told Christopher.

His voice broke Orange Fairy's train of thought, and she decided to ask her mother before speaking of such private things. Magic things their mother was not yet aware of.

"Both of you should go and wait with White Fairy. We will be along shortly."

Nodding yes, Orange and Yellow fairies flew quickly to meet their sister.

Orange Fairy turned around quickly, flew back to Myles and Christopher, and followed them toward their home.

"Is there something else you wish to say, Orange Fairy?" Myles voice echoed into the distance.

"Yes. First you do not need to keep saying fairy after our

names. Please just call me Orange. Second, I need a promise from you both to not speak of us to other people. We are already in so much trouble as it is, and when our father hears about this I shudder to think what sort of punishment he will mete out. Promise me."

"We have already given this promise to Yellow. You need not worry. We will not speak of this," Christopher assured her.

Nodding, Orange flew back to catch up with her sisters.

Myles and Christopher went to their homes, and gathered tools they thought might be useful to help free the princess. Since Christopher's father was the great builder, and sought after by many people for his skill, he had the better tools. They both ran so fast that they were out of breath by the time they reached White, Orange and Yellow Fairy. Dumping the large, leather bag filled with tools on the ground, they both stood with their hands on their hips, legs apart, and waited until they could catch their breath.

Then, after a very long, silent, moment, Myles forcefully spoke first, "Could you three explain something to me?"

With eyes open wide they waited for him to continue.

"Did you not know any better? And, because of that not knowing, explain why you fairies decided to take the princess out without telling someone, anyone? I am sure you know these woods are not always a safe place to play. They are far from the open meadow, and hold many dangers. What made you think it would be safe to bring the princess here? I have heard rumors of this Agnes, though I have never actually seen her. My father cautioned me about her, as she often walked around in a forbidden area. She constantly looks for strange herbs and poisonous wild flowers, and who knows what else. He said she is filled with anger and hatred for the king and queen. It is obvious to me now that she has pounced upon an opportunity to seek her revenge. I am sorry, but you should have told an adult, or your mother or father, what you were up to," He finished angrily.

"We did not know of this Agnes," Orange Fairy whispered.

"I do not understand how that is possible? Explain this to me."

Christopher cleared his throat and, touching Myles on his arm, said, "I think the reasons why the fairies brought the princess out into the meadow, and far into the woods on more than one occasion, no longer matter now—or that they were not aware of Agnes and her peculiar activities. What does matter is that we free the princess as soon as possible. And, Myles, we need to prepare for anything."

Nodding his agreement, Myles apologized to White, Orange and Yellow for his outburst, and continued speaking to them in a softer voice. "We can talk more on the way to your home, and…"

At that moment, Kim and the rest of the fairies approached Myles and Christopher.

Kim spoke in a clear voice. "My name is Kimberlyn, and these are my precocious daughters."

"I am Myles, and this is Christopher." Myles pointed.

The boys' shocked looks did not go unnoticed by Kim, but she continued speaking,

"There are few humans who know of the existence of our clan of fairies. I wish to keep it that way, Myles. I need a promise from you and Christopher that you will not speak of us to others. Do you agree to this?"

Myles smiled, and looked directly at Yellow and Orange fairies.

When Kim turned and looked at her daughters, she noticed Orange Fairy's face was turning several shades of pink and then red.

Looking directly back at Myles, she questioned, "Myles,

have you touched Orange?"

His eyebrows rose, "Yes. She was crying, and I wiped at her tears. I could not help myself. It was a natural reaction. I am not comfortable around women's tears."

"He called us 'womens'," Orange whispered to her sisters, and giggles broke out.

"If I have done something not permitted, I apologize, Kimberlyn."

"Although my full title is Kimberlyn, gold fairy mother, you may address me as Kim."

"Kim, I am sorry if I have done something wrong. Again, I apologize."

"You have not done something considered wrong but, rather, exceptional in its application. When a fairy is touched by a human for the first time as a gesture of kindness, they become bonded. Not like an acceptance or marriage, but rather like a merger of feelings, likes and dislikes. The best example I can give is in the behavior of human twins. You will begin to understand what each other is thinking and feeling. Your friendship will form and grow, as you grow to become adults. This bond cannot be broken, even in death."

Kim turned to Christopher. "Christopher, have you also touched one of my daughters?"

His sly grin had Kim smiling, but his words had everyone laughing. "No Kim, but I am thinking, perhaps, I could touch all of them."

As the laughter died down, she continued, "Let me get back to the subject at hand."

With a very serious look on her face, Kim said, "Now that we know what we are all up against, thanks to Pink and Zoo Zoo Piggy, dealing with Agnes might be a little difficult."

Kim took a moment to collect her thoughts.

"Because of her past behavior, she was banished by the king and queen. Much time has gone by since then, and I believe her mind has twisted itself with such hatred that her lies have become truth to her. Since the king and queen are friends of my clan, and we have met many times before, they must be told about this situation. They should be returning from their trip soon."

Kim continued, "Agnes' magic is powerful, but my magic…Forgive me, what I was about to say would appear to be boastful. Let me just say I know what to do, and I am prepared to do it."

Chapter Sixteen

Princess Teri fell into a fitful sleep. In the darkness, her nightmare flooded her mind and she relived the kidnapping.

Agnes had paced back and forth in front of her fireplace. Occasionally, she would look up at the princess, who was still in the arms of the giant rabbit. The princess had shaken with fear, and she had known that her sweet, kind, and loving Bun Bun Bunny had been under an evil spell.

Agnes had spoken in a low, cackling voice which had sent shivers up the princess' arms. "Rabbit, you are under my command to place the princess in the cage just outside this cottage. Lock the cage door, and return the key to me. If she tries to break free, choke her. Do you understand?"

The rabbit had just moved his head slowly up and down in his hypnotic-like manner, and had done as he was commanded.

He had taken four hops, had gone out the cottage door, and then had quickly placed the princess in the magic cage.

The princess had tried to run to the cage door before the rabbit could slam it shut, but she had been too slow, and had nearly caught her hands in the hard, cold steel. She had held on to the metal bars and had begun to cry.

Jerking awake, the princess realized tears ran down her face and, sadly, she was still cold, wet, hungry, and frightened.

With the key to the cage back in her possession, Agnes watched the bunny return to the large bed she had prepared for him. He fell fast asleep. She waved her hands in the air to ensure the bunny would not awaken, and then decided to take the key to a special hiding place where no one would find it.

She began to mumble to herself, "I do not understand why I have been so absentminded lately, but I must write this information in my Ledger Book of Accounts, else I forget."

In this book was written not only the location where Agnes had planned on hiding the key, lest it be taken from her, but it also contained anything relevant or important.

She turned around quickly, and spoke to herself again, "Where is that batch of poison I mixed yesterday to kill the weeds growing in my herb garden? Oh, there it is. I must add another ingredient before I paint it on my book—a safeguard if anyone should find it."

She clapped her hands together. "How delicious that would be if it were a fairy."

Her cackling laughter faded as she climbed down the handmade ladder to a dark storage room beneath the cottage.

It was here in this dark room that strange and, sometimes, complicated thoughts came to Agnes. The sound always began with a slow, deep, menacing, voice. Then it would be in her head, and it would become her own ideas and thoughts.

Agnes recalled the first time she had heard the voice.

As she had climbed down the ladder to the storage room she had held up a torch to look for old pots or cups. She had needed something large, but not heavy, that could hold all the herbs she had collected that day.

Although this storage room was well below her cottage,

and the ladder difficult to maneuver, Agnes was always happy to explore around, discovering old, planed wood, well-made fire-baked jars and plates, and an old trencher she used for holding rain water.

Agnes had continued searching, and had started up her complaints again about the queen. She had mimicked the queen's words with a scrunched up face, *You will be much happier here. You gossip and are overbearing. You tell the most outrageous lies. You cannot be trusted with a confidence.*

"Overbearing, indeed," she had said out loud.

You are not overbearing.

"What? Who said that?" Agnes turned quickly and, holding the torch higher, searched for the source of the words spoken so clearly, but saw no one.

She had decided it must be her mind playing tricks, and had continued her search.

You have every right to be angry. I can teach you things, show you things. Let me help you. You will have your day very soon, I promise. We need each other, can help each other. Let me help you Agnes.

The voice had stopped, and had entered her head where its dark thoughts continued to sooth Agnes, lulling her, changing her.

Snapping back to the moment, Agnes remembered how the idea of the poisonous concoction first came to her when she had made up her mind to take the princess.

However, the biggest surprise was her new abilities that made her witch-like, and she had conjured up the cage made from a material she knew could not be breached. That dark room, that sanctuary, was her favorite place to be and think.

Satisfied with her precautionary efforts, she went to her front door, intent on entering the Haunted Forest, as quickly as possible, to see to the creatures under her command once again.

Screaming Mirrorme glared at Agnes, who was shaking her head no.

"You think I do not know what you do here, Meme. I see the dead animal bones you have hidden. Pretending that you do not eat meat is insulting," Agnes said.

Mirrorme opened her mouth to send out her siren death call, but Agnes just laughed.

She pointed to her ears, and said, "I cannot hear you well enough for you to damage my brain. I am not stupid. I have my secrets, secrets to protect me from you, and from that giant of a worm. It has already agreed to help me protect this key."

Agnes pulled the large key from her cape pocket and waved it in a slow back-and-forth motion in front of Mirrorme's eyes, nearly hypnotizing the creature.

"I know your hunger is never satisfied with the little paltry meals you find for yourself," Agnes said. "I also know your ancestors once lived in the seas and feasted on fish, clams, shrimp and algae, and sang their siren songs to ships lost in storms. They enjoyed luring the sailors to their deaths. Some called your people mermaids, and they were described as beautiful creatures. But your people changed and adapted to the land. To this day, they continue the siren song of destruction in other lands, and have become eaters of men. I find your reflective face to be an amazing camouflage, and wonder if there are others like you."

Mirrorme shook her head no, then haughtily turned away waiting for Agnes to get to the point of her conversation.

"I understand you well, though you cannot speak. I know we can be good friends, and take care of each other. In return for your help, I will bring you people to eat, and you can protect me when I am here with you. I am prepared to give you a scrumptious human as payment. At this very moment, I have a girl, a princess, trapped in a cage outside my cottage. A very tall, lovely girl, with long, red hair and pale skin. She has large, green, liquid eyes with lots of meat to her bones."

Mirrorme started to drool. She lifted her head away, and crossed her arms over her chest once again to show Agnes she did not believe her. "I do not tell you a falsehood, Meme. I mean what I say."

Meme nodded her head in agreement.

"That is better. I need you to help me carry this goat to the cave. The creature there must stay distracted so that I may pass through to the other side. There is a tree that will protect this key in case you, the giant worm, and the creature in the cave fail."

Agnes continued telling Mirrorme her plans, and they walked slowly through the dark, Haunted Forest together.

When Myles and Christopher heard the echoing sound of the princess crying, Myles pushed Christopher's hand away from him and started running like a mad man through the woods toward her.

"Christopher, stop him. He will ruin all of our plans if Agnes sees him before we can get to her!" Kim yelled.

Christopher caught up to Myles, and grabbed him. They struggled for some moments until Myles realized his error. Myles apologized to Christopher and Kim, and in a tense whisper said, "I am OK, Chris. You can let go of me."

Christopher looked to Kim for reassurance, and then released his friend.

After composing himself, Myles looked directly at Kim, and said, "You have five minutes to deal with Agnes, before

Christopher and I start taking that cage apart piece by piece."

In a voice filled with strong confidence, Kim ordered, "Now, girls!"

Like a flying rainbow with golden glitter, the fairies burst into Agnes' cottage.

Kim stopped and looked around, only to discover Agnes was not home. "We must hide here, inside, and wait for her to return. Shhhh, be very quiet."

Myles and Christopher tried everything they could to get the cage door open. The princess had awakened, and was still shaking from the cold. She cried with relief seeing Myles and Christopher. Even Christopher's cloak couldn't seem to warm the princess, as she watched with concern the unsuccessful attempts each made to open the cage door.

"Chris, it is no use. This door will not budge," Myles said out of breath. "We need that key."

Myles looked at the tear-filled face of the princess, and spoke softly, "Do not worry, sweetheart. We will find that key and get you out of here."

Placing his hands through the bars of the cage, Myles held on to the princess's cold hands. His mind wandered back in time, remembering his first meeting with the princess and her parents.

"Do you remember the first time we met?"

"Yes," She said with sadness in her voice. Myles decided to help take her mind off the situation, and questioned her about their meeting.

"How old were we?"

"You know the answer as well as I."

"And?"

Princess Teri knew what Myles was doing, and smiled in

response to his cajoling.

"I believe I had just turned five and you were eight. My father was taking me to see his beautiful black stallion he had named Nicholas. He knew I was fascinated with the stallion, but that I was also afraid. So he lifted me up and put me on his shoulders. He was teasing my mother by pretending to drop me, several times, as I recall. The harder I laughed the more upset she became, and she made several attempts to pull me down."

Smiling at the memory, Princess Teri continued the tale. "I could smell the stallion as we went into your father's workshop, and I knew he smelled me, because he started prancing and snorting."

Her smile, now brighter, broke out into laughter. "I started pulling my father's hair because I was afraid, and he tried to hand me to my mother. But I stopped fussing because I saw you standing next to Mr. Albright, and you were looking at me. I do not remember talking to you, but I could not take my eyes from you. Finally, my father put me down, and you took my hand and we went out of the shop and played until my mother took me back home."

"Do you remember me asking your mother if you could come out and play again?"

"Yes. You know I do. And I think my mother was happy that I had someone close to my own age to spend time with. I do not recall many children around at that time, do you?"

"No. I met Christopher when I was nine, and I introduced you to him a year later. The point here is we have been together ever since. Nothing can separate us Teri. Not the abundant allergies or these bars."

Her tears glistened in her eyes, and she said, "I did not have many allergies then, but the rest showed up two years later. I remember being upset with my mother when she told me I could not go out-of-doors until the physicians figured out what to do.

And you and Christopher spent more time inside with me than you should have."

"I did not care where I was as long as I was with you. Even then, I loved you. At that first meeting, when our eyes met, I knew we were meant to be together."

Myles' words calmed her, and she watched him stand and go to Christopher.

In the comfort of her memories she closed her eyes and recalled Myles knocking on her door, and the first time she had met Christopher.

~

"Come in, Myles."

"Can you come out to play today?" Myles had asked.

Her nose had been red and she had been sneezing. "No, I do not think so, Myles. I am not feeling well again, and am told to stay inside."

"OK. How about I go collect my friend, Christopher, and we can have a great game of chess here in your room?"

"You do not want to stay in my stuffy room and play with me."

"Yes, I do, and when I beat you good, we can play hid and seek."

Princess Teri had followed him down the stairs as quickly as her allergies would allow. And, as they had sought out places to hide, the princess had wondered what Christopher looked like.

"I will be quick. Christopher would be very pleased to meet you, and angry with me if I did not include him." He had run out the door in search of his friend.

Weeks later, an idea had come to the boys, and they had been trying their best to persuade the princess to come outside.

"This will not work, Myles. I will suffocate."

"No, you will not. Just breathe slowly, and come outside with us."

"We are going to get into trouble, and you will be punished. I know you will."

"Look," Christopher said, "it will be just for a little while. Myles and I have been thinking about this for a long time. We are very good at solving puzzles and we think the air you breathe is a big part of the problem. Covering your nose and mouth should help a little, and you can be outside again."

That was the first day, after many long and sometimes boring days, that Teri was able to venture outside to enjoy the sights and sounds around her.

Myles and Christopher had given her a gift that day. Their gifts of friendship, love and determination would continue on throughout their lifetimes. Their constant presence and reassurance filled the princess with hope, and she could not imagine her life without them.

Chapter Seventeen

King Crawford and Queen Joyce returned to Fitzhuwlyn Castle with an uproar of activity surrounding them. All the servants were running around without paying one bit of attention to the king and queen.

The head butler finally saw the royal coach, and hurriedly walked toward them. They could see by his face that he was shocked by their sudden appearance. Perhaps the realization that they had arrived two days early was too much for the poor man.

The queen nodded, signaling Siomara, her lady-in-waiting, to investigate the situation. Siomara stepped from the coach, and walked to the butler.

She spoke in a soft voice, and asked, "Is something wrong, Mr. Williams? You look upset?"

Slowly taking his eyes from the king and queen's coach, he looked directly at Lady Siomara. Immediately, she saw the tears in his eyes, and patiently listened while Mr. Williams gave her the accounting of all that had taken place on this long and sad day.

"Lady Siomara. The most terrible thing has happened." He sniffed. "Our princess has been taken from us, and is a prisoner of our very own former servant, Agnes. I do not understand why she would do such a terrible thing. Do you think her mind has snapped?"

"I do not know, Mr. Williams. Please continue."

"Apparently, some little girls came and befriended the princess. They persuaded her to go out-of-doors so they could play.

On their returning to the castle, they somehow lost the princess. So they ran home to find their mother to help in the search."

Nothing was mentioned about fairies being the little girls. For none of the servants has actually seen them come and go.

"That is it. I know nothing else. I do not know how this happened. Most of us who work inside and outside the castle understand the princess has terrible allergies—life threatening allergies—and I, we, all worry for her health. We are all in the dark here."

When he had finished speaking, his face was red with anger and agitation, and Siomara did not realize that she had tears in her own eyes. She walked back to the king and queen's royal coach, and once again stepped inside. She sat down, and told them everything she had heard.

While the horses and coach were guided to the grooming barn, they walked toward the castle. With sadness in his eyes, and the weight of concern upon his heart, the king could not bring himself to look at his wife.

The queen spoke to Siomara after what seemed a very long moment of silence. "I have tremendous faith in my friend, Kim," she said. Once again there was no mention of fairies. "And I have no doubts about the abilities of Myles and Christopher to help our daughter escape the clutches of…I refuse to speak her name." Her voice shook.

Not knowing what else he could do to relieve his wife's sorrow, the king said in a very commanding voice, "I announce this royal decree that all in this kingdom are forbidden to say the name Agnes from this moment on. I hereby order that all subjects be banned from naming their daughters, pets, plants and fauna, rivers, creeks, homes or domestic serving animals Agnes. What I have said will be written, will be done."

With tears in her eyes, the queen turned to her husband and

nodded with satisfaction at this new law. She then spoke with a shaking voice, "Please dispatch a royal messenger, the quickest in the kingdom. Have him ask Myles and Christopher to let us help if we can, and to keep us informed of what happens at every possible moment."

When all had been done as the king and queen asked, all the inhabitants of the castle seemed to hold their breath for word of Princess Teri.

After returning to her cottage and hanging up her cape, Agnes decided to fix herself a meal, and rest a moment before checking on the princess. But Kim and her daughters were lying in wait. In a whirlwind of color, they flew at Agnes and pinned her to the floor before she knew what had hit her. They held on to her with all their might. Agnes struggled in vain against the power of Kim and her daughters.

She began screaming and shrieking at the fairies, "You think you can help the princess? Think again. I am more powerful than you can imagine. I have power only the dead speak of, and they quiver in their graves when I pass by. It is too late. She is probably dying from the cold and the damp rain falling upon her. Or her illness will become a slow torture, and she will die later. Yes, a slow death would be well-deserved."

Her anger aided her, and she broke free of their hold, running quickly to her front door with confidence of her escape.

Kim, with no time to think, rose up, reached behind her magnificent golden wings, and once again conjured up a fireball the size of a large cooking pot, and hollered, "On the floor, girls. Now!"

The flaming ball sailed through the air with great speed, and hit Agnes in her back. The explosion could be heard for many miles around, and the cottage shook with such a force the boards of the floor separated slightly, letting in the light of day between them.

After the smoke cleared, and the cottage settled back down, Agnes was nowhere to be found. Kim was breathing heavily while her daughters sat up, unable to move from the shock of it all.

"Mama," yelled all the fairies at once. They jumped up and flew into the open arms of their mother. After what seemed an eternity of silence, all the fairies whispered, "Where is she? Where did Agnes go?"

Kim looked at her daughters lovingly and said in a tired voice, "I sent her into Nothingness." She continued, when she realized they did not understand, "It is a place of holding where she will remain until I decide to free her. I believe she needs some time to herself to think about all she has done. Most importantly, she will not be permitted to harm another person or creature again. I am sorry that I did not keep an eye on her more closely. Had I been aware of her secret activities, I would have stopped her before things got out of hand."

Kim smiled at her beautiful daughters, and continued, "You are all so very young—babies really—and I promise to explain more about the misuse of magic when you are older."

After kissing them one at a time, Kim stared at the spot where Agnes last stood. Only the boards on the floor near the door showed signs of damage, blackened by the fireball. The air in the room seemed fresh and clean, with no odor of smoke lingering from the incident.

Kim spoke again, saying, "We must search this cottage for anything that will help us find that key."

They searched together, mother and daughters, with a determination to succeed in their task. Books went flying, dishes were thrown, and cabinets were emptied onto the floor.

Suddenly, Purple Fairy yelled so loud everyone's hearts

pounded and seemed to stop.

"I found her ledger. I found her ledger."

Kim removed the large ledger book of accounts from the shaking hands of Purple Fairy, and set it on a table.

"Listen to me very carefully," Kim spoke softly. "Today, we are going to use the speaking words of our language to help us understand what is written in this ledger. Come and place both your hands around the edges. Be very careful not to touch the symbol in the middle of the cover. I can see that it has been slathered with a poison more potent to fairies than humans."

The fairies approached with great caution, and stared unmoving at the leather-bound ledger. All were amazed at the intricate beauty of the gold and silver symbol.

"What does it mean, Mama, these crooked letters, arrows, triangles and stick people?" Red Fairy questioned.

"It is the symbol of death."

The fairies looked frightened for a moment, but nodded their heads for Kim to continue.

"As you can see, the crooked letters start and end the circle. They spell mourning, or sorrow. The triangle in the center of the letters represents the beginning, middle and ending of time, which I interpret as; the now starts, the middle has been set, and the end is unavoidable. The stick people drawn in the center of the triangle have the arrows pointing to their hearts. It means people will soon die of heartbreak because time will run out, and people will be the last tragedy. This is an ancient symbol and it is no longer used in the casting of spells.

"I do not know how Agnes forged this because it is made of only the purest of metals only a wizard can conjure. How she understands what she has created is beyond me. This symbol itself is a spell, but it must be said by the dark wizard who created it. I can see you do not understand my words, so I will explain this all later. However I do not wish to give you nightmares, so I will say that there are no dark wizards here."

Looking at each daughter with pride and trust, Kim nodded. All placed their tiny hands around the large, brown, heavy ledger that had every spell and accounting important to Agnes. They closed their eyes, and began speaking in the language of fairies. Knowledge from long ago enveloped them, and the latch that locked the ledger popped off. The book was open to a page with the information that Kim desperately needed. For the first time in what seemed like forever, everyone smiled.

Myles was seated on the ground in front of the cage once again, and held Princess Teri's hands through the bars. They spoke quietly to each other, while Christopher was busy digging under the magic cage looking for an opening.

He finally gave up, and said, "No use, Myles. I see nothing. No door, no opening, no way in. What in all the heavens is this thing made of?"

Kim and her daughters flitted up to the cage, and Kim told Myles, Christopher and Princess Teri what they had found in Agnes' cottage. Princess Teri could not take her eyes from Kim, and did not realize she was smiling at the beautiful adult fairy.

"So let me get this straight," Myles said. "The key to this cage is in a place called Haunted Forest. Christopher and I will be given three magic weapons by you, a magic sword, a magic ax, and a magic rope. Haunted Forest is behind your forest, behind these woods, in front of the meadow near the castle. Do I have that correct?"

"Yes, that is correct," Kim said.

"Why do we need these weapons?" Christopher asked.

Kim slowly moved away from the cage, determined to not be overheard by her daughters or the princess, who were deep in conversation. Myles and Christopher followed her.

"In her book, Agnes wrote of the many trips she had taken into the dark forest. Apparently, she has charged three creatures with protecting the key, and they do not care about people. I am familiar with these creatures. One is called Screaming Mirrorme. She is very clever and has a terrible screeching cry that can paralyze her prey. Second is Giant Worm. He crushes his prey, then slowly dissolves them. Lastly, is the creature hibernating in the cave. And just beyond that cave is a talking tree, where the key is buried.

"You must go through this cave and find the opening at the other end to get to the talking tree. Be as quiet as possible and let it sleep. This cave-dwelling creature is a very large creature—a creature of legend and folklore that breathes fire and eats anything living, but it prefers people. As long as it does not awaken, you should have enough time to fetch the key and come back from whence you came.

"But make no mistake, Myles and Christopher. If any of these creatures get ahold of you, they will torture you for sport before they kill you. Be mindful and cautious, and you should be back with the key before sunup." Kim said all this with a heavy heart. Myles and Christopher looked in the direction of the dark Haunted Forest then looked back at Kim.

Once again Myles spoke, "Since you are a fairy and, by your title, I assume a powerful one, why do you not go into Haunted Forest and look for the key yourself?"

"Because I do not love the princess the way you do. Agnes is not a happy person. She is a hater of love and all things good. I must remain here to keep an eye on her to be sure she does not escape the prison I have placed her in. And I will continue to check on the princess while my daughters keep her company.

Your love and Christopher's deep friendship for the princess is more powerful than any magic I can call forth. Love is a mighty force, Myles, and you are given a duty, a quest, if you will, to free the princess because you love her. My gifts are better used for keeping the princess safe and comfortable until you return with the key. Do you understand?"

"Yes, we understand." Christopher smiled at Myles, and nodded.

"I realize now that I would not have it any other way, Kim. Yes, we must be the ones to do this."

Christopher broke the seriousness of the conversation. "What are the chances, do you suppose, of another explosion like the one we heard back there?"

Kim tried not to smile and said, "I am really sorry about that, but I did what I had to do, and I am very proud of my daughters for their part in finding Agnes' ledger. It does not make up for the mistake they had made in bringing Princess Teri to the meadow so close to these woods un-escorted by an adult, but they are still very young and curious about people. Is there anything else I can do for you before your quest begins?"

"Yes." Christopher said quickly. "Is there some way you can give us, say, fairy protection or give us a drink to make us really tall?"

Myles and Kim burst out laughing. "Chris, you are already taller than I, and it is doubtful being taller will help much," Myles ended.

Kim gestured for Myles and Christopher to come closer together. "Close your eyes please," she said.

Myles and Christopher looked at each other, shook their heads, stood straighter, and did as Kim asked.

She stretched her arms straight up and called upon the

wind. She slowly began spinning around and around. Kim's wings branched out wide and tall, and in a quick, forward motion she flung her wings and arms straight out, directing fairy dust to hit its target, plastering Myles and Christopher from head to toe. The force of the air and fairy dust made them take three steps back.

When Myles and Christopher opened their eyes and looked at each other, they yelled at the same time with laughter in their voices, "Kim!"

Her hands went over her mouth, and the sound she made had Myles and Christopher smiling.

"I am so sorry," She finally said. "I think I got a little carried away, but I just want to make sure you are both covered well."

Myles and Christopher turned around, picked up the magic weapons Kim had placed there, and started walking toward Haunted Forest. Large clumps of gold fairy dust fell off of them with each step. Their hair sparkled in the glow of the setting sun, and the outlining shape of boot prints could be clearly seen going in the direction they walked. Kim could still hear them mumbling to themselves. As she started to leave, she tried very hard not to laugh.

As she approached the cage once again, she could hear her daughters' conversation with the princess, and smiled at her very words spoken to Myles and Christopher.

"Mama said when a fairy is touched by a human for the first time, they become bonded," Pink Fairy said in a breathless whisper.

"What is bonded?" the princess asked.

"It means we are your sisters, and are forever and ever."

Chapter Eighteen

Lady Siomara attempted to keep the queen occupied so she would not think so much about her daughter, but nothing worked.

After being told by their royal advisor, James, that it was not safe for them to go to the princess just yet, the queen could no longer concentrate on the duties of the kingdom.

Just when Lady Siomara was ready to pull her hair out, her brother, Jahaziel, walked into the lady's sitting room. She jumped up and ran into his arms, and gave him a huge kiss on his cheek. There was no mistaking they were brother and sister, so alike in features. Their dark, auburn hair, light brown eyes, and olive skin were striking, and made them stand out from other families in the area.

"I am so happy to see you," she nearly shouted. "The queen is beside herself with worry, and we have had no word from her friend Kim. I am frightened, Jahaziel, and afraid for the princess."

"Do not be," he said in a deep, yet pleasant voice. "I came here to see if there is anything I can do." Jahaziel slowly pulled his sister's arms away from his neck. He smiled down at her with a deep love reflected in his eyes, took her hand, and they walked toward the queen together. Queen Joyce looked up from her sewing, and smiled. After bowing to his queen, Jahaziel asked about the trip she and the king had taken, about the weather, horses and other minor things to keep her mind off the recent difficulties.

"You went as far as Goxfill and Skipfey, your majesty?"

"Yes, Jahaziel, and the weather there is always so pleasant. Crawford had heard of a new mare up for exchange, and wished to take a look. Once they agreed on the exchange of goods, he told me she was a gift for Humphries. As you know, his poor Miss Sugarspoon was so old she could no longer pull the supply wagon, and then she just decided to die on the poor man in the middle of a return trip," Joyce said, sighing.

"I remember Sugarspoon." Jahaziel smiled, "She was always poking me for treats whenever I tried to speak to Humphries."

"Mr. Humphries could not get his horse to wagon unless he brought her that spoonful of sugar, hence its name." After a hearty laugh from everyone, the queen questioned, "Did Crawford give you the saber, Jahaziel?"

"He did, Your Majesty, and I must say it is a beauty to behold. It has this ornately crafted design on the metal close to the handle. I thought it was something he had purchased for himself, but I was speechless when he presented it to me."

"Did Crawford tell you it was handed down from father to son for generations, and that it is rumored to have been forged by a great wizard, and that it holds unusual power?"

"Yes, and I believed not one word of it."

The sound of their joined laughter echoed out into the distance—laughter that was so needed in this time of great sorrow.

Princess Teri tried to be brave for the sake of the fairies, but she failed miserably. The princess sobbed softly to herself, hoping no one would hear her. When Kim came around the corner and heard the princess's distress, she flitted over to her and began to tell her about her life, where she was born and how she had become gold fairy mother. The princess was amazed at Kim's age.

"Fairies age slower than humans, and count our birth years with the passing of the moons. If I were to venture a guess by using your method you call one year, twelve moons, it would mean to you that I am somewhere close to forty-five years old. However, we assess thirty-six moons equal to one human year so, that makes my true age to be around 15 years. My girls have just turned one, which would be six by your count."

Princess Teri continued her questions, and this kept her mind off her problem, as she was very focused on the lovely tale. Even her daughters were enjoying the story and took turns asking questions.

"Our homes are built among a thick group of Cypress trees in varied shapes and sizes. Included in this design is a hot room for the drying of herbs and flowers often used for recipes, and for healing and the simmering of delicious soups."

Kim smiled at the attention and continued, "My father's name is Lutherian, and my mother's name is Glenlillian. Our meeting each other all started when I came upon a most-handsome, yet wounded, knight."

Laughter broke out, and Kim laughed along.

Kim continued on about losing her favorite walking plant named Patience, and to the princess's great surprise, told her she knew her when she was an infant.

It did not escape the princess's notice how much Blue Fairy looked like her mother more than the others, by her skin, hair, and eye color, and she wondered if Kim had a husband, and what he might look like.

Soon the princess began to yawn, and White Fairy pulled Christopher's cape snugly around her to keep her warm. Princess Teri finally sat down at a far corner of the magically built cage, leaned her head back against the wall, closed her eyes, and fell asleep to Kim's soft, musical voice.

Kim smiled that sweet motherly smile and turned to speak with her daughters. But Kim had to cover her mouth quickly so she would not make a sound. Not only had the princess fallen asleep, but so had all her daughters. They littered the floor of the cage like brightly colored flower petals scattered all about, with their tiny wings moving ever so slowly back and forth over their faces. Kim smiled to herself and wondered when her girls would grow out of that common baby habit of wing sing.

"No better than human babies sucking their thumbs," she said quietly to herself.

Kim flew back into Agnes' cottage and read her ledger once again. It was then she discovered Agnes' formula for creating a giant rabbit and, by fairy magic, reversed the process.

Satisfied he was his normal size once again, she picked up Bun Bun Bunny from his bed, went back to the cage, and gently placed him in the lap of the princess. Then she decided to take a nap herself.

Darkness came over Myles and Christopher as soon as they entered Haunted Forest. The eerie sounds they heard gave them goose bumps up and down their arms. But, unknown to Christopher and Myles, Kim had placed a special and magical gift in her fairy dust to fortify their courage and sustain their energy. Glancing at each other for just a brief moment, they nodded their heads, and silently walked in the direction Kim had told them to go.

They remembered Kim's words. She had told them, "Agnes' book states that you must not listen to the talking tree. It will try very hard to fool you into walking away from it. It does not want you near that key, and it will use reason, threats, curses and lies to make you stop digging beneath its roots. Listen to your hearts. Your love and determination to save the princess will help you find the key."

She continued, "Do not forget this very important step. As soon as you have the key in your possession, run. The talking tree will begin to collapse, and you will not have much time to get out of its way."

A loud, distant screaming seemed to come from everywhere. It shook Myles and Christopher out of their thoughts, and both covered their ears. Falling to their knees, they looked at each other, and knew that this was one of the three creatures Kim had spoken of.

Kim called her Screaming Mirrorme, and she was closing in on them fast. Christopher quickly threw the magic rope to Myles, and they both jumped to their feet, running in different directions. Christopher surmised that one more scream from the creature would surly rupture their eardrums, and death would be slow and painful.

Silent as a panther's stalk, they circled around and spotted her. They stopped in their tracks, and faced the dreaded Screaming Mirrorme. Kim did not tell them she was the most beautiful creature they had ever seen, but they remembered Kim's description of Mirrorme. Each was aware of her great ability to lie.

Her face was a mirror, and it reflected any image she desired. Merging the faces of Myles and Christopher onto her face, she managed to blend their image, change it, and make it hers. With confidence, she knew they saw what she wanted them to see.

They pounced upon her quickly.

"Chris, grab this end!" Myles hollered.

"Got it."

"Pull hard, really hard," he yelled again.

"May pole!" They shouted in unison.

In one quick motion, they wrapped the magic rope around her mouth, running in opposite directions of one another to quiet her. And then the fight began.

"Grab her hands, Myles!" Christopher hollered in a high-pitched voice.

"Hurry, I cannot hold on much longer."

Her strength was amazing, and she fought like a strong, wild boar. Grass, dirt, leaves and branches from the surrounding trees were flying everywhere. Dust rose so high it covered the tallest trees and seemed to get thicker as the fight continued.

At last, after what seemed an eternity of struggle, Myles and Christopher managed to tie her to a very large and old-looking tree. Their clothes were torn, and both were bleeding from different places on their bodies. Breathing heavily, Christopher asked, "Are you alright, Myles?"

"Oh, yeah," he said while trying to catch his breath. "One down, two to go."

As they both turned to Screaming Mirrorme at the same time, neither were surprised she had returned to her original form—ugly, old-looking, and slits instead of eyes, that gave her a monster-like appearance. Steam rose off of her body with every breath she struggled to take in. And she was angry.

"I do not understand why Kim comes to this place, as she said, now and again collecting things. What things could she possibly need from this area?"

"Chris, who knows why fairies do the things they do. But I am sure she has her reasons."

Checking the magic rope one more time to be sure it was secure, Myles spoke to the monster, saying, "Do not worry, I am sure Kim will be by sometime soon to collect her rope." Screaming Mirrorme opened her eyes wide, and both saw her fear.

"Yeah, I see you are afraid of Kim, gold fairy mother." Christopher shouted and used her full title as he finished his tirade.

"I bet she can whip your screaming, eye-glowering, ugly, fat. Yes, I say fat…"

"Stop, Chris," Myles said, laughing. "It is time to go. And just for your information, Mirrorme is not fat."

"I know, but it really made her mad, did it not?"

Christopher smiled with satisfaction, and both were assured that Screaming Mirrorme was secure. And, so they left the area and continued on their quest to find the key.

"You sure look awful, Myles." Christopher slapped Myles on his back hard enough to make him stumble forward. He then thought to speak of other things to ease their burden. He decided to tease Myles.

"I do not know who told you that you could be the boss of me, but you are sorely mistaken, my friend. I am older and obviously wiser by far. It is you who should be taking orders from me. I am a man, and look at you. You have a long way to go before becoming a man."

"Two months does not make you a genius, Chris. In fact it makes you quite the opposite."

Myles ran, and Christopher chased after him.

Myles always took the bait, and Christopher always ran. The happy sound of the boys' laughter echoed through the woods. The sound was not missed by the creatures residing there.

Chapter Nineteen

Jahaziel absently listened to the women talk, and he tried to decide if he should go into the woods to find Myles and Christopher. Sitting with the women was not his idea of giving assistance, so he made up his mind to go. He stood up, bowed to the queen, gave his sister a hug, and started down the hall toward the front doors.

"Wait," shouted Siomara. "Where are you going?"

"I thought to go down to the keep and practice with my men for a while. I am not good at standing around waiting, Siomara. You know that."

"Yes, I do. And you are starting to get on my nerves just a little," she said with a big smile on her face. "Do you think you could stop scowling like that? You are scaring the servants."

Jahaziel laughed, pinched his sister on her cheek, and walked down the hall, and out the large front doors of the castle. Jahaziel had no intention of going to the keep. He thought to himself, *no one has to know where I am really going*. Everyone will think I am somewhere else, and should not be looking for me. He decided to search for Kim, who he knew would have the answers to his many questions. He smiled to himself at the thought of seeing her again, and concluded for the hundredth time that it was a real shame Kim was a fairy.

Myles reached out his left arm and stopped Christopher from walking further.

"Shhh," he said. "Listen."

Christopher closed his eyes and became very still. They heard a low, pounding sound, like a drum. And there it was again—"boom." The rumbling sound, much closer now, shook the ground, and vibrated the trees. Hundreds of leaves fell from the trees making it look like rain that was colored gold, orange, brown, green, and yellow.

"Run!" yelled Christopher. "Run!"

Myles and Christopher ran like never before and, if their thinking was correct, they did not have much time before they would be crushed by the giant worm.

"There, up ahead!" yelled Myles, pointing and running at the same time.

Christopher could only follow behind Myles because it took all his concentration just to run his fastest.

Up ahead was a cave. Reaching it quickly, they stopped to catch their breath while looking cautiously at the very large, dark, damp, foul-smelling place.

"Please tell me this is not what I think it is, Christopher."

"'Fraid so, buddy. Dragon creature cave," he said in a quiet voice, almost a whisper.

Christopher walked closer to the entrance while Myles kept an eye out behind them. The booming sound, coming closer again, could be heard by the few woodland creatures who dared to venture into Haunted Forest. They scurried in confusion as to which way to go, and the birds started flying out of the trees. Christopher quickly covered his head as bats ejected themselves out of the mouth of the cave just ahead of the fire. It poured out of the entrance, and spewed forward a great distance, then sucked itself back in. Christopher quickly pushed Myles to the ground just in the nick of time. The flames shot out just inches above them, and little fiery sparks floated down, setting parts of their clothing on fire.

"Roll, Christopher!" Myles yelled.

They rolled and rolled, slapping themselves like fools. When the flames were out, they lay there and looked up at the sky, not moving, and barely breathing. And then they both burst out laughing.

Finally standing up, they looked at their arms and hands, reddened and tight feeling from the flames. Their clothes were still smoking.

"Wow, that was close," Myles said smiling.

"This isn't funny, Myles. We could have been cooked."

"No, I do not think so, Chris. Kim sprinkled a lot of that fairy dust on us, and I am sure it protected us."

"I see no humor here, Myles, so you can wipe that grin off your face right now."

"Hey, you were laughing too."

"Yeah, alright, I'll give you that."

"Well now, we need to decide what to do next," Myles said, looking at Christopher. And they both agreed. The Worm. So off they went again, following the now familiar sound of the loud thumping.

Kim woke with a start, her insight alerting her to the fact that Jahaziel was searching for her. She flew out of the cage without making a sound, and met Jahaziel halfway to Agnes' cottage. He stopped suddenly when he saw the sparkling, golden light of Kim shining in front of him.

His huge smile made Kim blush, and she stammered on in a rush saying, "I know why you are here, and I think it is a wonderful idea for you to help the boys. It has been some time since they left, and I have not heard from them. I cannot seem to focus my mind long enough to see where they are or if they are still alive. It is very dangerous in the Haunted Forest and…"

Before Kim could go any further, Jahaziel motioned her to come closer and covered her mouth with one finger to quiet her. Kim thought she would die of embarrassment, and she did not think her face could get any redder, but it did.

Oh my goodness, Kim thought. Jahaziel was the most handsome human male she had ever seen, and she was still a little smitten. The bond they had formed so many years ago continued to grow and, at each encounter, it became as natural as breathing.

"I am glad you have agreed to let me help Kim, but you should have sent for me sooner."

Gently lifting her left arm, Jahaziel looked at the ring he had given her so many years ago. She still wore it on her wrist like a bracelet, and Jahaziel smiled at the memory.

Kim smiled back and, speaking very quietly said, "There was not enough time to send this to you."

Jahaziel nodded his agreement and, speaking once again, said, "Would you like to sprinkle some of your magic fairy dust on me before I begin my search?"

"Have you been hanging around my mother? Magic fairy dusts indeed," she laughed heartily.

Kim nodded her head yes, and began slowly circling around him, and speaking so softly that Jahaziel had to strain to hear what she was saying. The golden dust was all over his head and jacket when Jahaziel opened his eyes.

A cloud of fairy dust floated in the air as he shook his head from side to side, while saying, "Are you sure you used enough of that stuff, Kim?"

They both laughed, and Kim followed Jahaziel until they came to the end of the woods, then they stopped at the border of Haunted Forest. Jahaziel's affection for Kim showed in his eyes and, leaning closer to her, he very gently tucked a little stray strand of her hair behind her ear. When he spoke, it melted Kim's heart. "You sure are the prettiest thing I've ever seen."

Then he smiled at her again, and questioned, "And where is Mr. Fairy?"

Kim burst out laughing, slapped him playfully on his nose, and said, "You know very well Huw is with my father, and will not return for a few more sun risings. Ah, what is your word? Days, is it? Did you not remember me telling you that very thing not one moon ago?"

Jahaziel nodded his head, but his smile faded as he said in a more serious tone, "If anything happens to me, send for the king. He will know what to do. Promise me."

"I promise, Jahaziel."

Kim placed a light fairy kiss on his cheek, and quickly flitted in the direction of Agnes' cottage, then changed direction.

Jahaziel stepped into the Haunted Forest in search of Myles and Christopher.

~

Kim waited until Jahaziel was far enough ahead that he would not follow her, or give her a dressing down thinking she was following him. Silently, she glided into Haunted Forest. Her intent was to seek out Screaming Mirrorme to retrieve her rope. She had no intention of leaving it behind.

"There you are, Meme. I see the boys have tied you well to that tree."

Mirrorme began to struggle, and Kim floated closer.

"If you promise me you will not seek out the boys I have sent here, I will untie you."

Mirrorme's thoughts raced, and Kim answered her question.

"I can hear your thoughts and, yes, I understand your promise. Let me just say this. If you try your screeching to harm me—by the way this cannot be done—I will send you to a place you will never escape from until I decided to release you. Do you understand my words, Meme?"

Kim's heart was moved by Mirrorme's tears, and she cautiously and gently removed her rope.

Thank you, Kim. This is not my fault. This is all Agnes' fault. She tricked me. She told me she would bring me a delicious human to eat—a girl human, a princess with red hair and soft, liquidly, green eyes. I am hungry. I have not fed in days. I grow weak even now. I could not fight you if I wished to.

Mirrorme rubbed her wrists, an attempt to return her circulation and to bring relief from the stinging pins and needles.

Kim closed her eyes and called upon fairy strength to hold back her anger. Then calming herself, she decided to save it for Agnes. She also made up her mind to demand that her mother crystal encase Agnes forever. She would hound her mother until she relented.

She took a deep, cleansing breath, and then spoke again, "I will take you to a deer that at this very moment dies from wounds inflicted by human hunters. It managed to drag itself into this dark forest, and suffers greatly. I will gently put it out of its misery, and you may have it to eat. It should last you awhile if you salt the meat and store it in a dry, dark place. I will collect the salt from the ocean for you, and bring it as soon as I can."

Why do you do this for me? Why are you not ending my life, here and now? Why?

"I wish you no harm, and ask a favor of you. No. Not like Agnes. Your screech can travel long distances if you go to your inside place. It can alert me of danger I cannot yet see. I need a heads-up, so to speak, of anything you regard as dangerous. Will you do this for me, Meme?"

Meme fell to her knees, and sobbed from relief. The fairy patted her back, and whispered kind, sweet words into her ear. "Hush now, Meme, everything will be OK. I can see we will be great friends. Shall we fetch you your food? I can start a fire quickly for you. You really should eat something."

All poor Meme could do was nod her head yes, and allow Kim to continue to soothe her. But she did not move. Her need for comfort and friendship outweighed her hunger, and she was so very lonely.

~

"I cannot hear you, Christopher!" Myles held his hands to his mouth and yell as loud as he could.

"The ax!" Christopher yelled again, and made a gesture of chopping down a tree. Myles, finally understood Christopher's idea, and they ran to a tree directly in the path of the slow-moving giant worm.

"One more, Chris, and that should do it." Myles was breathing heavily, having had his turn at the tree.

"Wait until he drops down, and then chop as hard and as fast as you can." He held up his hand and said, "Wait, wait." Christopher nodded and with ax lifted, he waited for Myles signal.

"Now!"

The cracking sound of the tree falling echoed through the forest, and the giant worm slammed his head to the ground, preparing to rise again in an effort to get out of the way of the falling tree.

The ground shook around them, and the loud booming sound echoed out into the open forest. The tree pinned the worm to the ground exactly as Christopher had planned, and they took their turns with the magic ax.

Myles and Christopher thought they looked awful before, but now, after chopping the tree and giant worm, they looked and smelled terrible.

Myles spoke in a loud voice so Christopher could hear him. "I am nearly done with these pieces, Christopher." He was fifty yards away, burying parts of the giant worm all over the Haunted Forest. Myles was chopping up what was left of the worm with the magic ax, assured that the many pieces would not turn into many worms. And both of them were clearly exhausted.

After he finished, Christopher walked back to Myles easily by the glow of the full moon, and he bent down to collect the last pieces. Moments later they heard what sounded like footsteps crunching dried leaves on the ground behind them, and they quickly turned.

With magic ax and sword in hand, they were ready to do battle.

Then they both hollered his name at the same time, dropped their weapons, and ran to Jahaziel, jumping on him so hard they knocked him to the ground. All three groaned with the impact. Then they both sat up, and began quickly talking at the same time trying to tell him everything that had happened.

"Whoa, slow down, gentlemen," Jahaziel said.

After catching their breath, Myles and Christopher took turns telling Jahaziel what had happened. Each agreed they could not fight the dragon, now awake and aware of their presence, without Jahaziel, the strongest knight in the kingdom.

King Crawford and Queen Joyce were so tired worrying about Princess Teri. They tried to sleep awhile, but could not, fearful they would miss news of their daughter when it came by messenger. They decided to take a walk around the castle and grounds, speaking with all their people as they went. It was clear on the faces of their subjects that everyone was worried about the princess. And some feared the worse.

Lady Siomara, on the other hand, decided to be cheerful and chose not to think bad thoughts. She asked the king and queen if she could organize a welcome-home event for the princess, and had many volunteers in mind to help.

Everyone thought that was a wonderful idea. Even the king and queen pitched in to help. Cakes were baked, meats were seared, banners were painted, and music was played—all in an effort to keep everyone busy.

Siomara saw a woman standing by the common well, wiping tears from her face with her apron. She walked over to her and spoke, "Sarah, I have been looking everywhere for you. I need your help arranging the dried flowers I have gathered for the table settings. Do you think you could spare me a moment of your time to finish this task?"

Sarah curtsied to Lady Siomara and, speaking in a quivering voice, said, "Oh, of course. I was just thinking that very thing."

Satisfied that Sarah now had a pleasant task to focus on, they both went in the direction of the hothouse to collect the flowers.

The sound of a flute playing in the distance had hands clapping to the rhythm, and soon servants and craftsmen joined in with dancing and singing. Siomara and Sarah tapped their feet to the beat as they sorted the dried flowers by color, and laughed in appreciation at a young man trying desperately to coax a young girl into a dance.

Satisfied with her efforts, Siomara walked back into the castle and into the small chapel situated to the left of the great hearth. She knelt down, and bowed her head and prayed for the safe return of the princess, her brother, Myles and Christopher.

~

With a plan now formed, Jahaziel, Myles, and Christopher headed for the dragon's cave. Jahaziel entered first, and took cautious steps, looking from side to side as he walked deeper into the cave, with Christopher and Myles right behind him. Then, out of nowhere came three floating lights, which flickered brightly behind them. Jahaziel turned around and walked to the dancing lights, ignoring Myles' yelling,

"No Jahaziel! It is a trap!"

He knew what they were, and stopped just short of the magic, floating torches. With his hands on his hips, he burst out laughing, leaning slightly forward as he did so. Waving a hand, he motioned to Myles and Christopher to come back to the entrance of the cave.

"What in heaven's name are those?" Christopher asked, pointing.

"A little gift from Kim, I suspect," Jahaziel chuckled.

"I have never seen anything like that in my life," whispered Myles.

"You have no idea the things that cute little fairy can come up with at times," Jahaziel said, more to himself than to them.

As each took a torch, and walked deeper into the cave, they were suddenly hit by unexpected heat. Perspiration immediately ran down their faces, making it difficult to see even with the aid of the magic torches.

"By all the heavens it is hot in here, Jahaziel," Myles spoke. Christopher nodded his agreement.

"It will get hotter as we get to the center. Focus on your task, and keep a sharp eye out. I have heard of this creature, this dragon, but have never laid eyes upon it. From what I have been told it is very large, swift, and wields a deadly flame it can call forth into a full, blasting inferno."

When Jahaziel stopped, Myles and Christopher nearly ran into his back. With magic torches lifted high above their heads, they could see the cave forked off into three, separate tunnels.

Jahaziel nodded, and each cautiously walked in different directions toward the tunnels. Myles went to the center, Christopher the right, and Jahaziel the left. Many moments passed before Myles reached the tunnel's end. Stretched out before him was the enormous interior of the cave that unexpectedly held a gigantic lake.

The water was not clear, and appeared to be as black as the cave walls. Christopher and Jahaziel ended up on opposite sides of Myles and so far away he could barely see them walking toward this lake of black water. Jahaziel quickly motioned to Myles and Christopher to not make a sound.

"Shhh," he whispered, touching his mouth with his finger.

The large interior of the cave seemed empty, but he knew that, in here, silence was important. He took his torch securely in his right hand, turned, and slammed it against the wall of the cave next to him, and motioned Myles and Christopher to do the same. The torches stuck to the walls of the cave without difficulty, and without making a sound. It was by fairy magic that this was done.

Chapter Twenty

Princess Teri was getting very tired of the fairies taking turns in telling her outrageous stories. She thought she was going to lose her mind if they did not stop and do something else. Zoo Zoo Piggy broke her train of thought, wobbled over to the cage, made a piggy noise, then hobbled through the bars.

The princess smiled and got down on her knees, as close as she could, "Hello again, little fellow."

Zoo Zoo Piggy got closer to the princess for a head scratch, making the little squeaking sound only guinea pigs made. The princess laughed, and lifted him up. She gently placed him on her lap. All the fairies floated over to the princess and the guinea pig, and smiled. He enjoyed all the petting and attention, but became distracted from his mission.

When Zoo Zoo saw Orange Fairy, he remembered why he had made the long journey, and scooted over to her to tell her something important. "Dododoo, Dododooo, Zuaaaha, Dododoo," said Zoo Zoo piggy.

Orange Fairy nodded, and thanked him for the information. When she looked up, everyone was looking at her.

"What?" she asked, while shrugging her shoulder.

Orange Fairy decided to keep her mouth shut and her thoughts to herself. Zoo Zoo had told her that Agnes was trying to use magic to manage an escape from nothingness. And, from the sounds Zoo Zoo heard, he was afraid she would succeed. Orange thought of a plan to ask Zoo Zoo to show her exactly where the sounds were coming from, and together they might find Agnes' prison—after which, she had to somehow convince her sisters to take turns guarding the area. No one noticed her and Zoo Zoo slipping out of the cage, or heard her mumble, "A fairy's work is never done."

~

Jahaziel, Myles and Christopher stared down at the lake of black water, and knew the dragon was hiding and waiting for its chance to attack.

Jahaziel made up his mind, put his hands to his mouth, and hollered, "In the water, Myles." He pointed at the black water, and continued, "Christopher and I will make enough noise to get its attention. When it comes out of the water, that demon dragon should be facing us. You must jump on its neck and thrust the magic sword into the back of its head. It is the only way to kill it."

Myles nodded, raised the magic sword, and braced himself for the fight to come. Christopher and Jahaziel pounded on the rocky walls of the cave and stomped their feet, while yelling nonsense things. They made a real ruckus.

Suddenly, the loud sound of rushing water echoed and bounced off the cave walls in a deafening roar. The dragon rose quickly, but instead of facing Jahaziel and Christopher, it was angrily facing Myles. The dragon let out an ear-piercing scream unlike anything they had ever heard before. With great speed, it was at the ceiling of the cave before Myles could blink his eyes. The fire came next. Spitting and moving its head from side to side, it covered the entire cave and lake in no time. When it was finished, yellow beady eyes scanned the cave for its dinner. But instead of finding the people burnt to a yummy crisp, it saw no one. Its eyes squinted and searched the cave again but saw nothing.

Jahaziel was first to come to the surface of the water, then Myles, and lastly, Christopher. They were all gasping for air, but ready for the assault from the dragon. In a quick motion, the dragon opened its huge wings and swooped down to the lake, breathing fire as it descended. Myles, Christopher, and Jahaziel dove back down into the water, followed by the dragon.

Myles knew being under the water would save them from the dragon's fire, and that was the dragon's mistake. Jahaziel thrust his saber toward the dragon's feet, forcing it to look at him and Christopher. Myles swam with great speed, quickly reached the neck of the dragon and, with magic sword in both of his hands, he thrust it into the back of the dragon's head so deep that only the handle could be seen.

The dragon shot out of the water in such rapid motion, Myles was not aware he was out of the water until his head hit the top of the cave, causing him to black out. He fell downward and back into the lake of black water with a great splash. The dragon screamed and threw its head from side to side, desperately trying to remove the sword. Using its claws and wings, it tried to dislodge the offensive thing. It quickly realized its end, and it glanced down toward its lake and spit out its last breath of fire—its hottest and cruelest fire ever brought forth. Jahaziel and Christopher dragged Myles out of the lake as the screams of the dragon made them look up.

"Run! Now!" Jahaziel shouted. "I have Myles, Christopher. Just run."

Christopher ran until he thought his lungs would burst. He surged out of the cave, and quickly turned around to see whether Jahaziel was coming with Myles. The fire exploded out of the cave a second time with such a force that Christopher was thrown backwards. His body was on fire again, and he rolled on the ground to put the fire out. He yelled all the angry words that came to mind. At length, Christopher lay on the ground smoking and resting. He mumbled, "This is the worst day I have ever had in my life."

Sitting up, Christopher looked at his hands blackened from

the soot.

"Oh yeah, ya think!" he raged.

Not expecting an answer, all he could do was wait. More moments passed with the realization that Myles and Jahaziel were not coming out. He stood up and walked reluctantly back into the cave, and tried calling forth his torch as he went, hoping he could remember his way back.

"Hello, little torch are you there? I need your help. Please come forth."

He couldn't help smiling as the torch came closer and hovered in front of him waiting for Christopher to take it. Now, with the torch held high above his head once again, what he saw took his breath away. Never before had he seen such total destruction. The walls of the cave looked as if they had been melted, and the once-jagged and pitted walls were smooth and shiny. The smell was that of sulfur and metal mixed, and steam was still oozing from the cave walls. Christopher walked until he came back to the lake of black water.

On the floor of the cave, close to the water's edge, was the large, lifeless body of the dragon. Its wings were stretched out so massively that each tip touched one end of the cave walls to the next. Its impaled head floated in the lake of black water, giving Christopher a clear view of the handle. The torch gently removed itself from Christopher's grip and joined the other two torches still stuck on a far wall.

Christopher heard strange, muffled sounds that made him look all around. Then, in that moment, he realized it had to be Jahaziel and Myles under the carcass of the dragon. He quickly reached them, and struggled for a few moments, and then managed to lift one of the large, heavy wings. Myles and Jahaziel crawled out from under it, breathing heavily. They stood up, and both started laughing so hard they fell back into the lake of black water.

"What is the matter with you people?" yelled Christopher, as he watched them climb out of the water again.

At last, when Myles could catch his breath, he said, "What in all the heavens above and the earth below happened to you? You're filthy, and the color of midnight from head to toe. All I can barely see are your eyes, Christopher. Did you fall into someone's cooking pit?"

Laughter again broke out, and Jahaziel desperately tried to speak, saying. "Christopher, you really should take a bath, man. And for the sake of your family, put your hair out." Loud peals of laughter followed.

Christopher, however, was not amused. He slapped his head like a mad man, and stumbled and fell to the ground with a hard thump. "You know, I have had about enough of you two, and you smell as bad as I look!" he shouted back.

Jahaziel, calmer now, finally stood, reached out a hand to Christopher and yanked him to a standing position. "Take your torches and leave them at the cave entrance for me. I will collect our weapons, then go back and tell the king and queen you and Myles are on your way to free the princess. You should have enough time to get the key from that stupid tree, and have the princess free by the time I reach the castle. Be quick about the rest of your business and remember how long the princess has been waiting, not to mention she must be sick with worry for both of you."

As he began walking away from the lake of black water, a sparkling red object caught Jahaziel's attention. After placing the weapons on the ground once again, he bent down, curious about what it could be. His surprise was evident as the object twinkled in the light of the torch still burning. There, before his eyes, lay a nearly buried, large, golden ring that held within the ornate design, a huge round ruby.

"I know this ring. It belonged to that gutter snipe, Arnault."

He pulled it from the dirt where it had clearly been hidden for many years. It came up with a boney hand attached to it. Jahaziel's laughter bounced off the walls of the cave and, speaking to himself again, said, "I always wondered what ever came of Arnault."

He jerked the ring off the boney finger, which fell into pieces when it hit the soft ground. Before placing the ring in his jacket pocket he spoke in a loud voice that echoed beyond where he stood, and continued out into the forest. "Your ring will be used to undo what you, yourself, destroyed so many years ago, Arnault. I will sell it and give the money, as payment, to the servants who lost so much in the fire at Castle Mead—the fire you set deliberately in a fit of anger. You destroyed homes and families with the intention of sending them into more than one hell. May this ring's profits bring a bit of peace and help to those who suffered at your hands. My bond as a knight, I swear this. And may you, King Arnault of no lands, receive neither help nor peace in the hell you are in now."

Lady Siomara was ordered by the queen to go to the cottage where her daughter was being held, to give her the basket that the queen filled herself. It almost overflowed with a dress, brush and comb, sweet-smelling soap, a container to collect water, drying cloths, blanket, slippers, cloak, fresh baked bread with cheese and succulent meats. She could hardly carry it to the awaiting coach. She stepped inside, and placed the basket on the seat in front of her while she sat in the other, and then signaled the driver to go. With the aid of the full moon, the view of the forest was clear.

Most disappointed in not finding her brother where he said he would be, Siomara mumbled, "I bet he left the castle and grounds without speaking to his men so he would not be followed. And if that is truly what he has done, I am going to give him a piece of my mind he will not soon forget."

The tiredness she refused to think about finally caught up with her and she fell asleep easily. The motion of the coach's rocking sent her deep into her dreams.

With a sudden jerk, the coach came to a stop. With horses whinnying, dust flying, and the driver yelling, Siomara jerked awake. She held her hand to her heart, and leaned out the window. Lo and behold, she saw her brother walking toward them. She jumped out of the coach, and ran to him, sprang up into his arms, and started giving him a piece of her mind, just as she had planned.

When the smell hit her, she jumped out of his arms, saying, "Jahaziel. What happened to you? What is that smell?"

Chapter Twenty-One

"OK, Chris, on the count of three, we run to the tree, dig as fast as possible, grab the key, and run like mad. Agreed?"

"Agreed."

"Remember, this tree is a master at lying. Do not listen to it."

"Myles, you have been telling me about this tree for the last mile."

Christopher smiled, slapped Myles hard on his back, and said, "One, two, three. Go!" They ran hard, and reached the talking tree very quickly. The tree was unaware of their presence, and Myles and Christopher started digging before it realized what was happening. The sudden voice from the tree startled them. It's high-pitched, nasally sound grew more and more distressed, but Myles and Christopher ignored it.

"You. Human. Stop. Stop I say. No, no, stop at once. I must tell you to listen. The princess is out of her cage. She waits for you even now. She worries for you. Go back to her home, and see for yourself. She calls your name and bids you come quickly. There is trouble there. Knights from another land captured her parents before she had returned to her home. And they wish to harm them. Do you hear me? Do you understand me?"

"Where in all the saints in heaven is that key!" Christopher yelled.

"Got it! Myles, run."

"No. Stop. Come back here with that key. You will kill me if you do not return. Oh, oh, oh, no, stop. I cannot…I cannot see. I dieeeee."

They took off running at breakneck speed and, immediately, the talking tree started breaking apart and into pieces. Its huge limbs were knocking the surrounding trees into each other, causing a domino effect. "Boom, boom, boom." One tree fell after the other. Myles and Christopher were not fast enough, and the weight of the talking tree's huge trunk pulled its enormous roots out of the ground. The sound, like a great storm of twisting wind, added to its sinister, monster-like appearance as it continued to topple. Knowing they were not going to make it, they looked at each other and prepared to die.

Kim saw Myles and Christopher running, and knew they would not make it on their own. She moved the magic rope above her head in circles, and flung it out to them. The magic rope wrapped itself around their waists and pulled them tightly together, and Kim quickly jerked the rope back to her. Myles and Christopher fell under her feet, and were knocked out cold.

Moments later, Myles and Christopher slowly opened their eyes and thought they were in heaven. Eighteen little hands were touching them all over their faces, and tingling sensations were flowing through their bodies. They smiled at the soft, whispering voices of Kim and her nine lovely daughters.

Then, in the flash of a moment, they were soaked from head to toe. They sat up quickly, and began coughing and coughing, and heaving in air as fast as they could. Jahaziel had dumped an entire drum of cold water on top of them, that just moments ago had been securely attached to the back of the royal coach. Its effect was exactly as he expected. Wide awake and completely drenched, Christopher and Myles could clearly hear the hysterical laughter all around them.

After everyone calmed down, Jahaziel spoke, "Myles,

Christopher, I am very proud of both of you. You have courage I did not expect in men so young. My men and I would be honored to have you as part of the royal regiment when you are ready, and willing enough to train."

He pointed, and said, "Over there is another drum of water for you to wash in, and a fresh change of clothing. The king and queen are no longer in danger themselves, and are with Princess Teri. The royal guards are posted and watching out for anything unexpected. Lady Siomara has brought the king's coach for us to all ride back in, and I am thankful my sister had enough sense to drop a few things off to the princess before we turned around to collect you. We are all beyond exhaustion, and I am thankful for the easy ride back."

He touched them playfully on their heads, and ruffled their hair. He then said one last thing before turning and heading for the coach.

"Be quick about it. Everyone is waiting."

Myles and Christopher nodded their heads and, as they walked to the water-filled drums, Myles picked up the magic rope and turned to Kim, "I see you found your rope, Kim. I hope you and Mirrorme had a nice visit."

She laughed at his comment, and continued to float next to Jahaziel.

"Wait, please, one moment," Siomara whispered, and she approached Kim, who was in quiet conversation with Jahaziel.

"Are you a fairy?"

Jahaziel looked at Kim, looked to the sky, and shook his head as he continued walking toward the coach.

Kim smiled at Siomara, "Yes, I am a fairy."

"Are those your daughters?" she pointed.

"Yes, would you like to meet them?"

"I would, yes please."

Jahaziel looked back, cleared his throat and spoke, "Ladies, can we make this quick, everyone is waiting for our return." And he laughed when he realized he was being ignored.

Kim signaled her children to come to her, and slowly introduced them to Jahaziel's sister.

With their eyes open wide, and with smiles upon their faces, each nodded to Siomara as their names were announced.

"Lady Siomara, this is Green, Yellow, White, Orange, Blue, Pink, Purple, Brown and Red. As you can see, they wear the colors of their name."

Kim laughed, and then continued, "I had nothing to do with that, and all these little moonkins can be very stubborn at times. I had beautiful names picked out for them when they first awakened and, as I slowly handed each of them over to their father and grandfather, I said their names. That was how I addressed them for a time."

With twinkling eyes, Kim pointed to each fairy. "Ahthuwin, Bonneisse, Cassahandra, Diafiena, Ellennin, Sharron, Miss Priss." Everyone burst out laughing at Purple Fairy's former name. Then Kim continued, "Lara and Esperanzia."

Siomara made a deep curtsy, and said, "I am very pleased to meet all of you, and I thank you for your assistance and bravery, as well as for your forbearance with this entire situation. My brother has filled me in on the circumstance of when and how this all began. But I do not chastise your children, Kim. I believe in my heart of hearts that all of this was not chance, but fate. I also believe we can be of assistance to each other, and work together in friendship—people and fairies. Do you not agree?"

Before Kim could answerer, Jahaziel poked his head out of the coach, looked directly at Kim and said, "Limiting your exposure to humans is now quite a moot point. Would you not agree, Kim?"

Kim smiled at Jahaziel, a warm smile that did not miss the notice of her daughters, nor of Siomara. As she spoke, a softness came to her voice, "And where would you and I be now had we not met, Sir Jahaziel?"

He thought a moment, then roared a hearty laugh. "Dead Kim. Quite dead."

Kim swiftly flew into the coach before Jahaziel could immediately react to Kim's plan to give him her what-for, but he was quick at grabbing her.

Siomara and the fairies stood transfixed at the sight before them, with their mouths hanging open in shock. The huge knight was tickling the fairy. And the fairy, with a giant of a yell was telling him to stop.

Princess Teri munched on the magic herb left for her by White Fairy, and paced back and forth in the cage making her mother and the royal guards nervous. She turned and looked out of the bars, and asked her one more time how she looked.

The smiling queen said, "You look beautiful." She reached through the bars and squeezed her daughter's hands, giving her more reassurance, then continued, "Besides, it never hurts to take the proper amount of time to make yourself presentable for the one you love."

Princess Teri's eyes opened wide as she looked at her mother with astonishment.

"Do not look so surprised. We all know you are in love with Myles, and he with you. I am sure Myles will be relieved that you do not appear any worse for wear, and that you have been taken care of to his satisfaction. Please try and sit down here, close to me, and let us talk about the preparations for your return home.

"All the people of Crawford Keep and Castle have been informed about everything up to this point. Teri, they are so excited and everyone is preparing a generous celebration. It has been far too long since we have had such fun. I think we should do this more often. Even Sarah has pitched in to help."

"Sarah? Shy, petite, flower girl, Sarah?"

"Yes. She and Siomara have made the most splendid arrangements. Oh, I was not to tell you this, it is to be a surprise. Please be surprised when you see them, or I am afraid it will break Sarah's heart."

The princess laughed heartily, and nodded her head in agreement.

"Mother, in spite of everything that has happened to me, I have come out of this for the better."

"What do you mean, Teri?"

"Well, I have met the most amazing fairy and her children. I am outside and enjoying myself because they defied their mother to help me by mixing an herb that daily continues to quiet my allergies. They are brave and silly at the same time, and I have more friends than I ever thought possible. I do not think I could ever repay them for their friendship and kindness. Mother, are they not the most magical creatures?"

"Yes, they are. Did you know Kim and I met just before you were born?"

"Kim spoke of this but did not go into detail. How did you meet?" Queen Joyce smiled a bright smile that went all the way to her eyes, and began her story with enthusiasm.

"You are not the only royal member of this family who has suffered at the hands of another. I, too, was kidnapped and whisked away from my home and husband."

Princess Teri was enthralled with this tale, and stared open-eyed, waiting for her to continue.

"I can see from the look on your face you do not know this story, so I will continue. Once upon a time lived a beautiful queen who…"

Princess Teri burst out laughing, and the queen joined in.

King Crawford could not be still, nor could he listen to one more complaint from subjects gathered in the royal woods with the makeshift assembly tent erected for their comfort and privacy. He couldn't bring himself to sit with his daughter and wife, while waiting for word from Sir Jahaziel. So he decided to hold court. His concentration, however, was not where it should be. And he felt this was indeed unfair to those gathered for judgments to have disputes settled, legal parcels of land researched, and his counsel sought. He cleared his throat, and spoke in a somewhat shaky voice.

"Please forgive me, but I cannot seem to concentrate. It would be a disservice to all of you here if I were to continue with this meeting. I believe I would like to take a walk, and anyone here who would wish to join me is most welcome to do so."

As the early morning dawn approached, and trees moved with majestic grace with the aid of a slow moving wind, the king could be seen walking with many of his friends and subjects in deep discussion of the common concerns of running a kingdom.

The sound of horses and trumpets could be heard in the distance, and all assembled knew that Myles, Christopher, Kim, her daughters, Jahaziel and Siomara were rapidly approaching. Even the forest creatures seemed happy and unafraid, and moved closer to the people.

As the royal coach slowed to a stop, Myles jumped out with key in hand and ran to the cage to release his princess. Princess Teri reached the cage door at the same time, and in that moment, Myles, seeing the look on her face, knew everything he needed to know without hearing her words. Love, joy, pride, and relief sparkled in her tear-filled eyes.

Queen Joyce spotted Kim, and walked to where she hovered.

"Kim, I am so very glad to see you again. And your daughters have grown since I last saw them. They are very beautiful."

"Thank you, Joyce. And Princess Teri is as lovely as ever. But I must take this opportunity to apologize to you for not thinking about helping Teri deal with those allergies sooner. When my children finally told me what they had done, I chastised myself for not thinking of it sooner."

"Kim, we have all been very busy with our lives and, if you recall, all of us, Crawford, King William, Sir Jahaziel, Sir Gauwain, and the servants of Castle Mead, agreed to not speak of our encounters with your clan. It would not have been prudent to let the rumors of the existence of fairies out to the rest of the world. Also, your apology is not necessary because Crawford and I had decided to speak with you about that very thing when we returned from our latest trip to the seashores close to Newry."

Joyce and Kim continued talking quietly to one another as the events of this exciting new day unfolded around them.

With shaking hands, Myles put the key in the lock and tried to turn it. The key would not budge. Myles looked to Kim with questioning eyes.

Coming forward, she spoke to Myles so only he could hear. "You must speak to the key, Myles. Your words must convince it to open. Use your heart to speak to it. And the love you have for the princess will command it to turn."

Nodding his understanding, Myles closed his eyes to collect his thoughts. Looking once again at Princess Teri he spoke slowly and with soft words.

He began, “My love for you is permanent; it does not come and go. The seeds were deeply planted into the recesses of my soul. For you, my love, have given me a gift beyond belief. A captured love, only you shall hold the key to its release. Each year passing, as it is grown, it is kept and held so sweetly. In its purest of forms your love adorns my heart and soul completely.”

Silently, the key turned in the lock, and the door opened, groaning in protest. Free at last, the princess jumped into Myles’ arms and started crying again. Queen Joyce, Siomara, Kim, and all her daughters were crying as well. Myles looked over at Christopher, Jahaziel and the king, who were clearly embarrassed by the show of emotion from the women and fairies. He said, “It must be a girl thing, all this weeping.”

Still holding the princess tightly to him, Myles waited for her to calm down. At last, when she collected herself, Princess Teri wiped her face with the cloth Myles gave her, blew her nose, and looked up at him ready to speak.

Before she could get her words out, Myles put his hands on each side of her face, lifted her head gently, and began kissing her on her forehead, her temples, her nose, her chin, and finally her lips.

They did not hear the loud cheering or the owl hooting, the rabbit hopping, the piggy squeaking or the horses prancing. Myles held his princess tightly to him until the sun slowly rose in the woods just behind the castle: The woods, where enough magic for one thousand stories existed just beyond the horizon. The woods, where all creatures and all fairies have lived for generations. The woods, witnessing the future wedding of Myles and Princess Teri, celebrated with joy and long memories. The woods, where it all began.

Epilogue

Egwin slowly receded from his hiding place, and took note from whence he came. It was time for another meeting with Farian and Linden. The Elvin Secret Society would come to session.

"I knew something was not right, Egwin," Linden spoke with a troubled voice, as he warmed his hands by the campfire.

"I thought we took care of this area last year? I am not looking forward to tangling with this darkness again."

"This is not the same thing, Farian," Egwin stated. "This is a different darkness. This is an old ancient darkness which now seeks release from its self-imposed prison. I believe it hides from us—or others like us—in that abandoned cottage. It is aware.

"I propose we set up some kind of schedule, taking turns keeping an eye on this thing. I do not know yet why it has decided to awaken, but be assured it has purpose and desire."

Egwin placed his head in his hands, and sighed.

"Your headaches have returned?" Farian questioned.

"Yes, just a few days ago, and I walked until I found the reason."

"This gift, or curse, you have never fails us in our search and mission of Destroyers of Darkness. Let me make you my tea, Egwin, it usually helps."

Linden rose, and removed the loose tea leaves he'd packed, and always kept handy. Pouring them into the clay pot filled with water, he placed it on the open fire.

"Ever since we tackled our first dark entity those many years ago, you have had these headaches. That thing clobbered you good, and all of us thought you dead," Farian recalled.

"If it were not for your father, Calvin, I believe I would have died, Linden. How is he by the way?"

"He is well, and very bored, Egwin. Transferring our escapades to the ledger drives him crazy. But, as he says, "At least I know what is going on." Then, as always, he tries to persuade me to take him with us to the next battle."

"Byron is the same," Farian spoke. "He tires of the constant repair to our weapons, and nearly begs to come with us."

"Our fathers know they would be more hindrance than asset if they continued the hunt. Sometimes I think they do not realize what a help they truly are. Their research alone saves precious time, and age seems to have sharpened their joined insight. They have not been off by much on the where, what, and whys of these dark entities, and the warnings they hail are near spot-on," Linden said with a heaviness he had not realized until this moment. He thought to himself how much he missed Byron, Calvin and Richmond's presence.

"Well, they do have each other, and their regular meetings keep them occupied and up-to-date with us," Farian said, smiling.

"I cannot thank Calvin and Byron enough for not only taking care of my father when we were away, but for making sure he comes to their regular meetings. Sometimes he can be a bit of handful when he is especially cranky and feeling sorry for himself. Please remember to tell your fathers how much I appreciate both of them," Egwin said.

"How much time do you think we have, Egwin?"

"I believe we have some time yet. Years maybe? My

headaches are tolerable, and come and go. That, to me, is an indication that it may be alone, and sleeps on and off. It may also decide to go back into hibernation where we cannot reach it. That's the only protection it has before a standoff, Linden."

"I cannot tell you how delighted I am to hear that, Egwin. I am still recovering from that last battle we had and, honestly, I do not have the strength to do battle again so soon."

"I know exactly how you feel, Farian. I agree with you, and I am sure Egwin does as well." Linden handed Egwin his tea and questioned, "What if it is not alone? Should we tell her?" Egwin shook his head no, intent on not including Kim. Their shared silence finally broke, and they continued their conversations and preparations for a future battle yet to come.

"Is that you, Egwin?"

"Yes, Father."

"Did you remember to pick up my supplies from Rolland?"

"I did, and I will make you something to eat straight away."

"You are a good son. Call me when you are finished, and I will set a place for us outside by the overhang."

Egwin loved the large ancient oaks, and knew his father had built their home for the shade they provided, and for the secrecy. It was a grand place to live and be.

He thought often about searching for Meirionwen, Diamond Fairy Mother, for she alone possessed the kind of magic that could remove his father's blindness. His last fight with a dark evil ended its existence, as well as Richmond's sight.

Meirionwen was called forth by Calvin to heal Egwin those many years ago. The head injury had left him paralyzed, blind, deaf and unresponsive to their shouting for him to wake. Or, so he was told after his healing.

He did not know for sure if she could help his father, or indeed if she was still alive, but he needed to try. To do something, anything, was better than seeing his father suffer so, year after year, unable to see his beautiful land and home. It broke Egwin's heart. But he did not know where to go to find her, and decided to speak with Calvin on the matter, and seek his advice.

As he prepared the meal, his mind traveled back in time to the first moment Richmond mentioned what he and his two friends really did when they were away for long periods of time.

"Egwin, you are old enough to start accompanying me, Byron and Calvin on our trips. Byron will be bringing along Farian, and Calvin is bringing Linden. We are having a meeting of our society tomorrow night at the round oaks meadow. From now on it will be your responsibility to ensure we have ample supplies of food at each meeting. Farian is bringing extra water and horses, and Linden with be carrying a few weapons of sorts.

"It is time you and your friends joined us to follow your destinies. It is a continuation of the blood line, eight generations now, of our three families, which formed a bond in ancient days that cannot be broken.

You three will go through training exercises, and a trial period that will hone your skills to perfection. Once Byron, Calvin and I are satisfied with the results, you will be given the weapons that have been passed down from father to son. You, and you alone, will have the ability to wield only that weapon given you. All three of you must agree to all that is presented to you and, from that moment, you will be responsible for the care and well-being of each other. Do you agree to this, Egwin?"

"Yes, Father. I agree to all you have said."

"Good."

Richmond placed his hands on the top of his son's head and spoke in the ancient language of the elvin people, "I, Richmond, Destroyer of Darkness, member of the Elvin Secret Society, do hereby present my son, Egwin, as member and apprentice of the new generation of Destroyers of Darkness."

The End

About Therese Grant

Therese Grant spent her childhood and teen years in Cleveland, Ohio where she enjoyed the company of her large family. Included in this wonderful menagerie of family were many aunts, uncles, and hoards of cousins. As large families often did in those days, they would gather at one house or another to cook, eat, drink, celebrate, and tell outrageous stories.

Often, when the children gathered together in attics, basements, or out-of-doors, a contest would begin, and a winner was declared after the most outlandishly frightening stories were told. The happy screams of children could be heard echoing up and down the stairs, long hallways, and into the streets.

This began Therese's introduction into the art of fantasy storytelling. Shy by nature, it would take her several years before she would brave an audience. Always losing to a better storyteller, she nevertheless persevered, and never gave up on the idea of creating a great story.

Therese resides in Columbia, South Carolina with her husband and family. She is constantly surrounded by many of her loveable pets.

CPSIA information can be obtained at www.ICGtesting.com
Printed in the USA
LVOW13s1951220614

391177LV00001B/1/P